Praise for Ashley Little's

"Lovers of youth, tats, junkie stories and street will come to love Ant and the prick he's trying not to be. PRICK is not cheap flash. It's all custom-made: Ant's high tat art on fast-forward."
—Cathleen With, award-winning author of *skids* and *Having Faith in the Polar Girls' Prison*

"Fearless, the straight stuff! An arresting look at the world of tattoo; graphic as a freshly embroidered skull on virgin skin. With wistful shades of Willie Vlautin and all the grit of Charles Bukowski, Ashley Little lushly demonstrates that hers is an important new voice in unflinchingly real story telling."
—Dennis E. Bolen, author of *Kaspoit!* and *Anticipated Results*

"Ashley Little's debut novel is so real and raw that you'll forget you're reading fiction. All the world really is a cesspool in this intense cautionary tale. Readers will watch with horror as Ant makes one bad decision after another: I devoured his story in a single sitting."
—Angie Abdou, award-winning author of *The Bone Cage* and *The Canterbury Trail*

"Ashley Little's debut novel is a brutal and compelling tour of the tattooing world's underbelly. Let me be the first to say, PRICK really gets under your skin."
—Teresa McWhirter, author of *Some Girls Do* and *Dirtbags*

confessions of

Tightrope Books 2011

a tattoo artist

by Ashley Little

Tightrope Books
17 Greyton Crescent
Toronto, Ontario
M6E 2G1 Canada
www.TightropeBooks.com

Edited by Shirarose Wilensky.
Cover design and typesetting by Karen Correia Da Silva.
Author photo by John Harkin.

This is a work of fiction. Any resemblance of characters to actual persons,
living or dead, is purely coincidental.

Produced with the support of the Canada Council for the Arts
and the Ontario Arts Council.

Printed in Canada.

Library and Archives Canada Cataloguing in Publication

Little, Ashley, 1983-
Prick : confessions of a tattoo artist   Ashley Little.

ISBN 978-1-926639-38-3

I. Title.

PS8623.I898P75 2011   C813'.6   C2011-901248-0

ONTARIO ARTS COUNCIL
CONSEIL DES ARTS DE L'ONTARIO

Canada Council
for the Arts

Conseil des Arts
du Canada

For my friends who were in the right place at the right time—
And to the memory of those who weren't.

I don't have a lot to say. I just want you to know that I'm sorry. For all of it. I don't even remember how to do this. Okay . . . alright.

Forgive me. Forgive me, for I have sinned. It has been seven years since my last confession. These are my sins:

I abandoned Grace, my grandma, in Calgary. I left her with Grandpa Seth. He abused her. And I let him. They raised me. I fucked off as soon as I finished grade twelve and didn't look back. Moved to Victoria. Can't say why exactly. I liked the idea of living on an island, detached from the rest of the world. I had no idea what I was gonna do when I got there, had about a hundred bucks to my name. Alls I knew was that I had to get away from him, from them, and Victoria seemed like as good a place to live as any.

Drawing was the only thing I was ever any good at, unless you count getting in trouble, getting beat up, getting high, and getting girls. Usually, when I'm drawing, people leave me alone, and I like that.

I've always had a fascination with tattoos. Can't say why exactly. Maybe because it's one of the only clear details I remember about my parents. They died in a roller coaster accident at the West Edmonton Mall when I was three. I stayed with Grandma and Grandpa for the weekend. They told me that Mom and Dad would be coming home with all kinds of presents for me from their trip, *if* I was a good boy. And I imagined all the toys and candies and colouring books and kites and water guns and G.I. Joes I'd get when they got home. But they never came home. Grace told me they were gone forever. And I didn't understand that. I didn't even know what forever meant. I thought maybe I'd done something wrong and they'd decided to go live somewhere else without me. Maybe they would get another little boy and he would behave and he would get all my presents. Grace told me they had gone to live with God in the Kingdom of Heaven. I thought that sounded alright and that I'd like to go live with God in the Kingdom of Heaven too, but Grace said that I couldn't go there, not now, not for a very, very long time.

Both my parents had tattoos. Mom had a red rose with thorny stems wrapping around her ankle. Dad had a black ship at full mast, sailing over his heart. I remember loving their tattoos, wanting to peel them off and play with them, pressing my arm or my chest against my dad's chest, hoping that ship would somehow transfer on to me.

I grew up in Forest Lawn, North Calgary, and I was flying with a sketchy bunch of hoods. We'd get forties of OE, smoke copious amounts of weed, skateboard, steal CDs, steal cigarettes, steal bikes. We'd steal money out of vehicles, vending machines, parking meters. We'd jump people in back alleys and take their watches and wallets. We'd steal cars and go joyriding or street racing. We'd cruise down Electric Ave. and whistle at the whores, and when they came up to the car we'd tell them they were too ugly for us, that we'd rather fuck a dog, then we'd laugh and spit in their faces and take off. We'd go spray-paint random shit and count how many days it took for the city to cover it up. We'd go to punk shows at the Multi and sell oregano in little Ziplocs to idiot kids for twenty bucks a bag. We were always looking for mayhem, and when we couldn't find any, we'd make it. We made Molotov cocktails, fake IDs, and honey oil, rocket launchers, pipe bombs, and five-foot bongs out of PVC pipe. One Halloween we dropped pumpkins off the Anderson overpass and caused a thirteen-car pileup. We called ourselves "The Droogs" because we were obsessed with *A Clockwork Orange.* I tried every drug I could get my hands on. By the time I was sixteen, I'd done pretty much everything but heroin.

I was sent to AADAC in grade ten when I got busted for selling pot at school. In AADAC I got more interested in tattoos. I began to recognize them as a sort of armour. No one fucked with the guys with big tattoos. The ink somehow made them tougher, wiser, more powerful than the rest of us. I began drawing and designing tattoos in a big black sketchbook that Grace gave me for my birthday. It had thick, creamy paper, and about two thousand pages. I still have it somewhere. It's all filled up now.

....

When I moved to Victoria I didn't know a single soul. I just knew I wanted to live there, surrounded by beaches and beautiful women. I got a shitty little room above the George & Dragon and worked there as a dishwasher for way too long. It was a ratty hole, but I met a few cool people and we'd usually smoke joints and have beers together after work. It was an easy job, I got free meals and dirt cheap rent. I couldn't complain.

I'd been scoping out tattoo shops in town and managed to save enough to get a couple small pieces done: a scorpion on my left shoulder, a black dragon on my right calf. I always tried to start up conversations with people who had tattoos, without seeming like a creep-o. I'd find out where they got them done and what their experience was like. I'd heard good things about Hank the Tank at Capital Tattoo on Broad. Hank had done my scorpion, which was my first piece, and is still one of my favourites.

On the afternoon of my nineteenth birthday I walked into Capital Tattoo, all gutsy and shit, eh. There was no one in the shop except Hank, and he was sitting behind a big wooden desk, drawing with a purple felt. He looked up briefly when I walked through the door, then went back to his drawing. He didn't recognize me, even though he'd done my scorpion only a month ago. I took that as a good sign, meaning he had lotsa clients. I looked around the shop for about ten minutes. It seemed clean enough, black-and-white tile floors and black walls. There were two black tattooing chairs in the main part and a closed-off room at the back for private work. There was a waiting area with a black velvety sofa and two black chairs and a table covered with tattoo magazines and a photo album full of tattoos Hank had done. Racks of flash lined two walls and the flash was okay, as far as flash goes. Lotsa traditional stuff, and some of the more modern crap: tribal armbands, barbed wire, Kanji characters that mean peace-love-dream-best-friend-forever. Or something. Some butterflies, some pin-up girls, some cartoons, some more butterflies.

"Something I can help you with?" Hank grumbled. His bald scalp shone in the light.

I walked up to his massive desk. "My name is Anthony Young. I want to apprentice with you," I said, looking him straight in the eye, not blinking, not moving, serious as a fucking heart attack.

"No. Fuck off." He went back to his drawing.

I stood absolutely still. Hank continued drawing, totally ignoring me. I don't know how long I stood there, maybe thirty seconds. Maybe a minute.

"Are you deaf, kid? I said FUCK. OFF."

"I'm going to learn to tattoo and I want to learn from the best. You're the best."

Hank looked me up and down, snorted. "I can't pay you," he said.

"That's okay."

The phone rang. Hank didn't move. I didn't move. The phone rang.

"Well," he said, "that phone's not gonna answer itself."

I grabbed the phone from beside his jar of pencil crayons. "Capital Tattoo, Ant speaking."

The person on the other end wanted me to make a donation to their charity for cops with cancer or dogs with cancer or police dogs with cancer, something like that.

"No, I don't want to. No, not in the future, either. I want you to take this number off your list." I hung up. Hank mumbled something I couldn't understand. He crushed a cigarette into an overflowing ashtray. His ashtray was made from a human skull. A sign on the wall behind him read:

ABSOLUTELY NO SMOKING. MINORS AND INTOXICATED PERSONS WILL NOT BE TATTOOED UNDER ANY CIRCUMSTANCES. NO CREDIT, DON'T ASK. WE ACCEPT CASH ONLY. TATTOOIST RESERVES THE RIGHT TO REFUSE ANY TATTOO FOR ANY REASON.

"Okay, sit down here, boy. Let's have a little chat." Hank lit another cigarette and offered me one from his pack, nearly empty.

"Ant."

"Eh?"

"My name's Ant. Or Anthony, if you like," I took a cigarette and Hank flipped a Zippo in my face, then lit his own.

"Whatever. Listen, kid, *if* I decide to let you apprentice under me you will need to follow my rules. Can you follow rules?"

"Usually."

"Not good enough. Get out." He turned around and started sifting through some papers.

"I meant that usually I can follow society's rules, but I'm sure I'll have no problem following your rules." I sort of felt like I should call him "sir," but I couldn't bring myself to do it. I cleared my throat instead.

Hank made no sign that he'd heard me and started looking something up in a binder and jotting stuff down. After about five minutes he turned around to reach for the ashtray. I think he was surprised to see me still sitting there. He grumbled something about the mother of a goat and crossed his huge arms over his chest, leaned back into his chair. He did not look impressed that I was still sitting there, and I half expected to be forcibly removed. He stared real hard at me for what felt like a hundred years but was probly only a minute. I did not look away.

"Alright, rule number one: I'm the boss."

"Right."

"Rule number two: I. Am. The. Fucking. Boss. Got that?"

"Got it."

"I make the rules and you do not question them. Whatever I say, goes. I'm the owner. I'm the main tattooist, and I'm your boss. And I will make your life a living hell if you decide to piss me off."

"I won't."

"You already are, now stop interrupting me. Rule number three: Don't interrupt me."

"Okay."

"What did I just say? Jesus, fuck. Rule number four: No one gets refused a tattoo. For any reason. There're gonna be a million assholes coming in here who want the stupidest shit you've never imagined and you're not gonna want to do it. You're not gonna want to even *think* about doing it. But you *are* gonna do it because that's why you're here. To practise. Right?"

"Right."

"Why are you here?"

"To practise."

"You put the ink on. They pay. I'm tryin to run a business here, so if you start beaking off to me about morals or karma or permanence or any of that hippie bullshit, you're out on your ass. You do not refuse one single tattoo while you're working here. Is that clear?"

"Yes."

"Me and the other artist here can pick and choose, alright? We've paid our dues. If we want to refuse someone, that's our prerogative. The only reason you will ever refuse someone a tattoo is if they're under eighteen or piss-assed drunk. Why? Because drunks bleed all over the place and it's a goddamn bloodymother mess to clean up. They're not worth your time or my hassle. Do you have a problem with alcohol?"

"No."

"Drugs?"

"No."

"Good. Because I like both." He laughed.

I laughed.

"No one gets tattooed on credit. We take cash only. No refunds, returns, or exchanges, because . . . ?"

"A tattoo is forever?"

"Bingo."

"What about trades?"

"No trades! Cash! Hard cash! And nobody gets a price drop. Nobody gets a discount for any reason. Not your girlfriend, not your best friend, not your mother."

"Okay."

"If anyone whines about the price, direct them to the sign on the till." He pointed at the cash register:

GOOD TATTOOING'S NOT CHEAP
AND CHEAP TATTOOING'S
NOT GOOD.

"How do you determine price?"

"Good question. Most of the flash is marked, but if they want it in a difficult spot, like say the ass crack or something, then we add twenty-five percent. If it's a custom piece or a combination of different flash or a cover-up, you figure out whatever you think the price should be, double it, and add fifty bucks. That's how you arrive at your subtotal, and then you get to add HST on top of that. The very, very minimum base charge is fifty-five dollars. That's for even just a tiny fucking little speck of a black dot, and that's just for the hassle of getting out your ink and setting up your station."

"Sounds good."

"Oh, it's good."

"Where did you do your training?"

"In Surrey, Nanaimo, and New Zealand."

"How long have you been tattooing for?"

"Longer than you've been alive."

"Cool. So, where do we start?"

"You're gonna start by sweeping the floor, mopping up, washing the windows, taking out the garbage, and cleaning the toilet. You'll be answering the phone and getting my coffee. Your name will be Shop Bitch, and you won't even come close to tattooing humans for ten to twelve months, maybe more."

"Seriously?"

"Do I look like I'm fuckin joking?"

"I just thought..."

"Don't think. I'm not paying you to think. In fact," he laughed, "I'm not paying you at all." He got up and went to the sink and poured himself a glass of water. "What'd you think? You were just gonna waltz into a shop and start tattooing?"

"Well, not exactly."

"Not exactly, not exactly." He screwed his face into a pout. "Exactly not, you fuckin moron. Alright, let's see your portfolio."

"My . . . oh. It's at home."

"Christ's chewy cunt, are you mentally retarded or something? What'd they do? Send you over from the mental institution? Here, look, take this back to your people," he pulled a toonie out of his pocket and held it out to me, "and tell them not to send any more of you fucktards over here."

"I can go get it, I'll be right back."

"Don't bother. You've wasted enough of my time already. Go home, kid. Playtime's over." He walked to the door and turned the SORRY, WE'RE OPEN sign over to CLOSED.

I grabbed a blank sheet of paper and a pencil from the desk and started sketching a skull with a dagger going through it and a snake coming out the eyes. Hank stood out on the sidewalk for a while, smoking, watching chicks come out of their yoga class across the street. He came back in after a few minutes and loomed over my shoulder. I thought, *He could kill me right now and no one would ever know.* But I didn't stop drawing.

"Let's see a mermaid."

I flipped the paper over. Hank watched while I sketched her outline. I could feel his breath on the back of my neck and a shiver ran down my spine. Then he sat down behind his desk and rolled up his sleeves. His arms were covered with skulls and daggers, man's ruin, a hula pin-up girl, FTW, traditional stuff that looked like he'd been wearing it a long time. I wondered what else he had that I couldn't see. He opened the top drawer, pulled out a big baggie, and started to roll a fat joint.

My mermaid's body was pretty sexy, but I couldn't get her face right. It looked pinched, rat-like. There was no eraser on the pencil, so I smudged her face out with my thumb and started over.

"Nipples, more nipples." Hank sparked the j.

I nodded. This is gonna be alright, I thought as I looked at the Harley Davidson clock on the wall behind him. It was 4:20.

"So, what are your hours?"

"Whenever the fuck I feel like opening till about . . . now."

"Do you take walk-ins or is it by appointment only?"

"Nah, it's mostly walk-ins. People don't bother making appointments anymore. They've got no consideration for my time, my schedule. There's no such thing as common courtesy left in the world, you know?"

"I know."

"No, you don't."

We laughed. Hank's laugh was coarse, like gravel scraping on pavement. His teeth were yellowed from nicotine and he was missing his right canine. He had a short, pointed beard that looked like steel wool. He was built like a refrigerator, which explained his nickname, Hank the Tank, or simply, Tank.

I pushed the mermaid across the desk to him and he handed me the joint. He studied her for a very long minute. In my head I chanted: *Please let him like it, please let him think it's good. Please let him like it. Please let him think it's good. Please.* Hank cleared his throat, then rolled his chair back, put his feet up on the desk. "Well, I guess I got me an apprentice," he said. We shook hands. I was grinning like a shit-eating fool but I couldn't help it. *Thankyouthankyouthankyou.*

I noticed the bluish LOVE HATE tatts on his knuckles and figured he'd done time, but I never asked him about it.

"What about infibulation?" he asked.

"What?"

"Piercing."

"Not interested."

"Good man. That shit's for gay homosexuals, if you ask me. You're not a gay homosexual are you, Ant?"

"Nope."

"You sure?"

"Nope."

"You're not sure?"

"I mean, no, I'm not gay. Definitely not."

"Good."

"So you don't do piercing here then?"

"Can you read? Can you see that sign? CAPITAL TATTOO. Not Capital Tattoo and fucking gay ass piercing. Fuck that faggy shit."

"Right."

"Alright, kid, that's enough jibber jabber for today. If you still want to apprentice with me and remember you're not gonna see a bleeding red cent for any of your work for about a year and a half, maybe two, and you better believe I'm gonna make you do all my dirty work then come back tomorrow at the crack of noon. Bring three

ashley little

10

prick

grapefruits, three bananas, three potatoes, and a stack of paper plates. And don't be late."

"Sure, what for?"

"We're gonna have a fuckin tossed salad, what the fuck do you think?"

"Will do," I said, heading for the door.

Hank grumbled something mean, I didn't catch all of it.

I turned around, "Oh, Hank?"

"What?"

"Thank you."

....

I walked down to the harbour. The sky was grey. The ocean was grey. Leaves and litter floated around in little swirlicues on the sidewalk. I took a photo of a tourist couple for them and didn't even think about taking off with their expensive-ass camera. I was going to learn how to tattoo. I hummed a song I didn't know the name of and didn't even like. The white lights outlining the legislature building twinkled, and for the first time I noticed the little gold man on top of the middle spire. A man and his bayonet. Made entirely of gold. It reminded me of a story Grace used to tell me for bedtimes when I was little, about a king who became miserable because he got what he wished for: that everything he touched turn to gold.

....

I realized I hadn't called Grace all month and that she would probly want to talk to me today, my birthday. I walked around downtown for about an hour looking for a payphone. But there are so many goddamned junkies in Victoria that the cops took all the payphones away, thinking that would somehow put an end to all the drug deals going on. But druggies could conduct deals through carrier pigeons if they had to. Nothing's gonna get between them and their next score. No phones? No problem. Work out some telepathic shit with your dealer. Bang out some Morse code with some church bells. Hook up some tin cans and string. Nice try, piggies.

Finally, I found a phone booth outside a Rotten Ronnie's but someone had ripped the receiver off, so it was about as useless as a nun's cunt. So I figured I'd go find a bar and have a beer or three to celebrate my birthday, now that I was legal drinking age in BC and all. Then maybe I could use the phone at the bar to call Grace.

In six blocks I passed about a thousand junky bums with their hats out. One thing living in Victoria has made me good at is saying no. If I gave a buck to every crack head outta work outta luck broke-ass beer-guzzling bus-fare-hustling gas-huffing fund-raising filthy-stinking dog-fucker who asked me for a dollar, I'd be fifty thousand dollars in debt and they'd be one hit closer to an ugly headstone. Fuck that gutter scum. I've got better things to do with my loonies, like try to land em between the sweet cheeks of strippers, or crazy-glue em to the pavement outside the G&D so I can laugh at all the suckers who try to pick em up. Now that's cheap entertainment.

....

I found a funny little bar to have a drink. The walls and tables and ceiling were covered in a wild collection of bras, panties, foreign currencies, and photo IDs. Drivers and hunting licences, student cards, bank cards, and status cards with strange, confused young people staring out from the identification they'd left behind.

The bartender was wearing overalls with no shirt, which I found mildly disturbing, but he seemed to fit in with the décor. I gave him a 100% tip to ensure that I could use the phone to call Grace later on. I took my beer to the back of the bar. There were only two other people in the bar. Two crusty old drunks with mesh trucker hats and plaid shirts, counting out their dirty change on the table, laughing too loud, coughing too much. I could hear the phlegm rattling around in their throats and it disgusted me. I sat silently sipping my beer, thinking of who I could call to come help me celebrate. There were some guys from the kitchen I'd had a few laughs with at work, but I didn't have their numbers. There was the hot server, Carmen, but she would still be working for another few hours. There was the other server, Natalie, but she was kinda bitchy. There was Brett, the guy I bought weed off, but he was strictly business. There was that cute girl from the bagel shop, but I didn't even know her name. So that left . . . no one. There was no one who would come. I drained the last swallow of my beer and went up to the bar to use the phone.

"This phone is only to call cabs or 911," the bartender said.

"It's my birthday. I want to call my grandma."

"That's nice."

I wanted to kick his crooked teeth in. I wanted to slam his skull into the bar. I hated him and his stupid overalls. I wanted to reach into his tip jar and take my $5 back.

"Please," I said through clenched teeth, hating, hating, hating.

"That's better." He handed me the phone.

I let it ring about a thousand times. Finally, Grace picked up. She sounded like she'd been sleeping, or crying, or both.

"What's wrong?"

"Anthony! What a surprise! Oh, nothing, sweetheart, everything's fine. How are you?"

"Good, good. I'm nineteen now."

"Oh, that's right! Happy birthday, dear."

"Thanks."

"Anthony, you should call more often. We worry about you."

"I don't have a phone, Grandma." I glanced at the bartender, he rolled his eyes. I hated him.

"Oh, I see."

"So, that's why I can't call."

"What are you doing for work, honey?"

"I got a job in a tattoo shop. I'm studying to be a tattoo artist."

"Oh dear."

"What?"

"Tattoos are for criminals and prostitutes, Anthony. Nice people don't get into that stuff."

"That's not true, Grandma."

"I pray for you, Anthony."

"Thank you."

"Do you go to Mass out there?"

"No. Not lately. How's the old man?"

"He's . . . he's not . . . he's not that good."

"Oh?"

"Well, he's sometimes losing his memories."

"Oh."

"Would you like to speak with him?"

"Actually, I have to get going now. I'm using a phone in a restaurant."

"Okay, dear. You're out with your friends, I suppose?"

"Yeah."

"Well, you have a nice time with them, now."

"Yeah, I will."

"And, Anthony, call us again soon. We love to hear from you."

"Okay."

"May God bless you, Anthony."

"You too. Bye."

The bartender's back was turned. Fuck him. I grabbed my five bucks out of the big stupid tip jar and walked out into the street. The air was cold and wet. Whores were whoring, bums were bumming, hustlers were hustling. The smell of ninety-nine-cent pizza was too good to pass by. I ate three slices under fluorescent lights, watching the grease pool onto the paper plate, turning it transparent. Then I went home, got into bed, jerked off thinking about Carmen, came spectacularly, and slept for eleven hours without dreaming.

....

My first day apprenticing with Hank, I knew that I wanted to tattoo for a living. Imagine getting paid to draw skulls and naked chicks on people. It was pretty much my dream job.

Everyone who came in the door was at Hank's mercy. They had to be good enough for him to tattoo. If he thought they were a poser, he'd ignore them until they eventually left. The clients idolized him. They took all his suggestions to heart. They wanted to please him with their tattoo ideas. As if the tattoo was for him and not for them. It was obscene. Of course, not every client was like that, but the ones that weren't usually ended up going elsewhere to get their ink.

Hank showed me around the shop: where he kept everything, what everything was, what to do with it, how to clean it, how to put it together and take it apart, and where it belonged. The ultrasonic cleaner and the autoclave were kept in the back room, which was strictly off limits to customers.

"Unless they absolutely insist on seeing it, then and only then can you take them back here. But don't let them touch anything! I work clean, alright? I may be a dirty MF but I work clean and I keep my shop clean and everything is safe as fuckin safety scissors. Some guys work dirty. They have autoclaves and sterilization equipment set up in the front, but it's all for show. They never actually fuckin use it."

"Really?"

"Yeah, really. That's just wrong if you ask me. It's wrong and it's wrong and it's wrong."

"I completely agree."

"If people want a dirty tattoo they can do it themselves with a goddamned Walkman motor and a goddamned guitar string. Hell, they can go to any prison in the country and get better tattoos than a lot of fuckin scratchers on the outside are charging big bucks for."

"Yeah?"

"I don't have a lot of morals, and I don't get uptight about much, but I am a professional, and professionals respect the tools of their trade. The needles are clean. The bars are clean. The tubes are clean. The machines are cleaner than Mr. Clean's shiny balls. The stencils are sterilized. The motherfuckin chairs are sterilized. Everything is sterile and clean, alright? Look at this soap. Look at this isy. It's not for show! It's almost gone!" He shook the bottle of rubbing alcohol in my face. "I've gotta order more. Oh, hey, you can do that." Hank turned away from me and walked over to his ashtray, picked out half a cigarette, and lit it. "I absolutely will not tolerate laziness or forgetfulness in this department. This is a legit business and I won't be shut down because some dumbfuck like you forgets to clave his needles or wash his hands, right?"

"Right."

"Can I trust you?"

"Yes."

"I guess we'll find out." Hank picked up a box of black gloves and threw it to me. "Gloves. Wear new gloves for everything and throw them out when you're done. Use as many pairs of gloves as you want. Wear a pair for setting up your station and then change them when you start the actual tattoo. If you pick your nose or your ass while you're doing a tattoo, change your gloves. If you're gonna take a drink of water while you're doing a tattoo, take your gloves off. Wear gloves for everything except handling money and answering the phone. Wear your gloves all the time. Just get used to wearing the fuckin gloves, okay?"

"Okay."

"Try some on."

I snapped on a pair. They felt pretty good. They looked pretty good. "They're nitrile. Not latex. Never use latex. Latex is shit. It's thin, it rips, and some people are allergic to it. Did you ever meet anyone who was allergic to latex?"

"I don't know."

"Me neither!" He laughed and clapped me on the back. "And Vaseline! Make friends with Vaseline." He opened a jar and smeared a glob on my cheek with a tongue depressor. "We use tons, literally tons, of this shit. It's good. It helps the ink run smoothly. You'll see. We like Vaseline. We like lube of all types. But Vaseline is best. For tattooing that is." Hank winked at me.

I wiped my cheek with my sleeve.

"Needles!" Hank grinned a maniac grin and held a bunch of needles wrapped in cellophane up to my face. "A big part of your job will be putting our needle groupings together for each day. Different configurations of needles do different things. You got your fine liners, thick liners, round liners, your round shaders, your flat shaders, your flat magnums, your curved magnums, and your massive motherfuckin magnums. Needles are soldered onto bars," he held up a bar, "with flux. It's like crazy glue but better. Bars go into tubes and tubes go into the machine." He put a grip assembly together and handed me a machine. "This, my friend, will be your machine well, one of them."

I felt the weight of it in my hand. It was smaller than I'd imagined, but heavier than I'd expected. It was silver and shiny and perfect.

"And I never want to hear you call it a gun," Hank said. "Guns have bullets. Machines have needles. Guns are for killing or wounding. Machines are for tattooing. If you want a gun, go look in the bottom left hand drawer of my desk. Only hacks and idiots call them guns. A tattoo machine is not a weapon. And if it is, well, maybe you're in the wrong business. How do you like your coffee?"

"Black."

"Good. Get two of those and one with cream and sugar. Lotsa sugar cause I ain't too sweet." He smiled, showing his missing tooth, handed me a ten. "When you get back you'll meet Sonya, her tattoo name is Shadow cause she don't say much. See ya in five."

I walked across the street. The air outside was misty and smelled like coffee and seawater. There was a big lineup and the chick behind the counter looked like she didn't give a fuck how long people had to wait, she was gonna make their coffee in her own sweet time. She was small and cute but had really short blue hair and was probly a dyke. The lady ahead of me ordered a single no fat caramel latte extra hot, no foam, half caf, and the blue haired girl rolled her eyes at me. I smiled. I got three large coffees and a lemon poppy seed muffin because I'd skipped breakfast and was suddenly starving. I gobbled it down in two bites before returning to the shop.

....

A tall woman with long black hair stood talking with Hank when I came in. She was so beautiful that she made me feel sick. She was wearing combat boots, jeans, and a black T-shirt that said PRETTY GIRLS MAKE GRAVES. She had colourful quarter length sleeves tattooed on both arms and I couldn't wait to find out what else. Her tattoos were gorgeous. I could see flowers and waves and fish and stars and birds without staring too much. She had black and purple makeup around her eyes. Her eyes were blue and pure.

"Hey," she said. She looked a little like Bif Naked, but sexier.

"Hi."

"Sonya, Ant. Ant, Sonya. You two will be working together."

We shook hands. Her hand was warm and strong and full of silver rings. She smiled quick and tight and then went into the back room.

"Don't get any ideas," Hank said, shaking his head. "She's not for you."

I could feel the heat rise up my neck, into my face. I've always been teased for blushing, curse of the carrot tops. I turned away and went to the can so Hank wouldn't see my embarrassment.

I decided early on not to give Hank any ammo he could use against me. I wanted only to take from him whatever I could learn about tattooing and then fuck off. I didn't want to work for him. I didn't want to be his friend.

....

November rolled by like a freighter on the horizon. I was learning tons of new stuff every day at the shop and washing dishes at the George every night. I was making just enough to cover rent and some food. I got a free dinner every night I worked at the pub, which helped a lot. I was basically Hank's slave and Sonya's lackey, but as Hank was fond of saying, "If you want to make tattoos, you gotta pay your dues." So I kept cleaning, sweeping, mopping, disinfecting, sterilizing, sterilizing, sterilizing, autoclaving, booking appointments, placing orders, cutting stencils, making needle groupings, getting coffee, getting croissants, getting cigarettes. I kept drawing.

I learned not to talk to Hank before he'd had his morning coffee and cigarette. I learned not to talk to Sonya unless I had something important to say. Sonya didn't do small talk. She didn't talk much about her past, or about anything, really, which made her somewhat of an enigma, which I think was what she was going for. I learned that she'd apprenticed under Gotsie Shorman in New York, which explained why she was so damned good, if a bit on the snobby side. But damn those snobby bitches always got under my skin. Like they just knew they had something I wanted, and it was something I would probly never have.

Sonya hated doing necks and hands and referred most public skin to Hank. Hank referred everything he didn't want to do to her, and eventually both of them referred anything neither of them wanted to me. Sonya didn't much like doing flash either, but the fifty-five dollar rose and the hundy butterfly paid her bills, so she'd do it and try to put her own special flair into it. When someone came in with a sweet design and asked her to do a custom piece, her eyes sparkled and you could tell that's what she really lived for. That's why she was there.

As far as I knew, she was the only female tattoo artist in Victoria, and she was building a good name for herself and a fine rep in town and beyond. I had to snicker when people asked for her by her tattoo name, "Shadow." I just thought it was the cheesiest thing since cheese strings and could never take it seriously. *Who knows what evil lurks in the hearts of men?* THE SHADOW KNOWS*!!!* Mwahahahaha!

Totally ridiculous, right? I mean, who gets away with that lame bullshit anyway? Well, Sonya did. She had a good chairside manner with clients too, better than Hank anyways. If Hank didn't like someone's idea for a tattoo, he told them they were an idiot and to get out of his shop. If Sonya didn't like someone's idea, she casually tried to convince them to morph it into something more acceptable. Sometimes it worked, sometimes it didn't. She was very persuasive, in her way.

One day a cute chick with glasses and blond spiky hair came in wanting a tribal design on her lower back. You know, ass antlers. Hank rolled his eyes and sent her over to Sonya.

"Okay, your design is pretty cool, but you don't really want a tramp stamp do you?"

"Excuse me?"

"Placement is just as important as design. Everyone gets this spot tattooed, it's overdone. It's not original anymore. In the industry, we call this a tramp stamp."

"Really?"

Sonya nodded gravely.

"Well, I've thought about it a lot and I want it there."

"What if I change the design a little bit, make it end up in a spiral here and we place it above your hip, on the side here, see, so it fits the natural curve of your body?"

"Yeah? I don't know . . ."

"I'm just gonna change the shape of this part." Sonya began drawing out a new design.

"It's my tattoo. Shouldn't I get to choose where it goes?" She looked at me for help.

I shrugged.

"Of course, of course you should. Absolutely. Just think of me as your artistic advisor. I really just think you're much too unique to have a tramp stamp."

The chick smiled. "Thanks, I guess." She probly wanted to bang Sonya just as bad as I did.

"I'm gonna go make a stencil. I'll be right back."

The chick sat on the pleather waiting chair, gnawing at her nails, knees bouncing with anticipation.

I swept the floor, sneaking a look at her tits every now and then, which were barely concealed under a thin pink shirt with flared sleeves. Led Zeppelin played on the stereo. Rain pattered against the window. Multicoloured umbrellas floated past the shop. She picked at a hole in her jeans. I stood by the door and lit a cigarette and stared at her, fully aware that I was making her uncomfortable.

Sonya burst back into the waiting room and showed her the stencil. The chick liked it even better than her original design. Go figure. Sonya glanced at me, making sure I was getting all this. She soaped her, shaved her, applied the stencil, fired up the machine.

Forty-five minutes later, that chick walked out with a tattoo she didn't even know she wanted. And she left Sonya a huge tip.

"The Shadow strikes again," I said, as the door closed behind her.

Sonya smirked at me. "Hope you're takin notes, Antsy pants." She had some gift. Some power. Some amazing influence. I wanted it too. And I wanted her. Oh God, how I wanted her.

It took me almost four months to get up the balls to ask Sonya to give me a tattoo. By that time I was tattooing potatoes, grapefruits, bananas, and paper plates pretty much every day. Paper plates were the hardest, but they taught me to work with depth. Bananas were difficult too because of their mushy guts. But I had made some goddamned gorgeous grapefruit tattoos.

"Tattoo yourself," Sonya said.

"I want it on my back."

"Use a mirror."

"She's a tough bitch, eh, Hank?" I lit a smoke. Shot down.

"That's why I hired her."

"How are you even gonna pay for it? You don't make any money." Sonya took a sip of her coffee.

"I could repay you with sexual favours."

She spit her coffee back into her cup and started coughing and laughing so hard I was scared she might choke or puke or both.

Hank keeled over his desk, laughing his raspy, gravelly laugh.

"What?"

They both laughed and laughed at me while I sat smoking, studying the hairs on my forearm, my dick shrinking by the millisecond.

"I don't see what's so hilarious about that," I said.

"I'm gay, Ant." Sonya said.

"Oh." I couldn't tell if she was fucking with me or not. I decided that I didn't care. It didn't matter anyways.

"She's right though, kid," Hank said, suddenly sober. "You're ready to tattoo yourself."

"I am?"

"Choose a small design and put it in a discreet place."

"This oughta be good," Sonya said. She went to the front, turned the SORRY, WE'RE OPEN sign over, and locked the door.

"I don't know, I . . ."

"Hey, Ant, don't worry about it," Hank started rolling a joint. "If you fuck up, all you have to do is forgive yourself."

"Yeah, I guess."

"And if you really hate it, you can always do a cover-up job later, then you'll learn how to do a cover-up. It's all about learning right? Practise, fuck up, learn, practise some more."

Sonya held up one of my grapefruits, examined it in the light. "Is this supposed to be a straight line?"

"Yeah."

"Is this supposed to be a circle?"

"Uh huh."

"You'll be fine." She threw the grapefruit at me and it hit my chest with a thunk.

"Why don't you go home and sleep on it," Hank said. "Come back tomorrow around four and we'll see if you've got what it takes. Here," he tossed the joint to me. "Maybe that'll give you some inspiration."

I walked out, jittery, light-headed. I realized I'd only had four coffees, a deck of smokes, and a croissant that day. And that probly wasn't enough. I wasn't working at the George that night though, so I couldn't get my free dinner. I had three dollars in my pocket. I got two slices of meat lover's pizza and sat at the window, watching people go by. Gawky couples holding hands, guys out looking for girls, guys out looking for fights, guys out looking for drugs, guys out selling drugs, regular-looking chicks who were all whored up, wearing short skirts and heels and gobs of makeup and shit. After awhile of watching red and pink dresses skank by, I realized it was Valentine's Day. That most sleazy of cheesy, shitty Hallmark holidays when anyone with legs, and even those without, can get laid. It had been awhile for me so I walked over to the bank, took out twenty precious dollars and headed down to The Sticky Wicket to see what I could get myself into.

There were heaps of sparkly chicks there, all of them single, all of them young, willing, and able, all of them consuming alcohol. I had nothing to lose.

....

The secret to picking up a girl is you gotta let her come to you. Cause if you approach her with some lame one-liner, then you're just some creep-o, trying too hard to pick up, and she'll get creeped or irritated and fuck right off. But if you let her come to you, well, then you've got the upper hand. Cause then she thinks she's the one in control of the situation, thinks she made the choice to engage with you, and if anyone's a lame loser in that scenario then it's her, cause she came on to you! You can't lose that way.

....

I baited my hook with a cold beer and sat quietly at the bar with the joint tucked behind my ear, making sure to keep the stool beside me open, making some suggestive eye contact now and again, letting those sweet little fishes swim right into my net.

When there were only a few inches of beer left in my glass, this lady came up to order a drink. "Gin and tonic please, and," she turned to me, "what are you having, sweetie?"

She was a cougar. Probly forty or something. She was not ugly but she was old. She wore a tight red shirt and jeans that showed her camel toe. She was wearing pigtails that looked wholly ridiculous. But her eyes were soft and sad like an old dog and I thought, Aw, what the hell? She bought me two more drinks while we shot the shit, neither of us really listening to the other. Then I asked if she wanted to go smoke the joint with me somewheres, and she smiled and took me by the hand, led me out the door.

Her apartment was in Chinatown down a tiny little back alley that you'd miss if you blinked. It was a pretty neat little place with high brick walls and tall, skinny windows and a loft. I could imagine myself living there, drawing, painting, looking down on the street below, maybe getting some plants or fish or something. She made us some pink tea which she said was herbal and enhanced sensual pleasure. We sat by the window, smoking the joint and sipping that awful tea. Then she took her socks off, and pulled her shirt over her head. I stared at her breasts through her lacy bra and thought, This is too easy. I cupped her chin in my hand and kissed her hard on the mouth. She took off my jeans and socks and shirt and I had to climb the ladder up to the loft wearing only my underwear, which made me feel stupid, like a stupid little kid, being sent to bed. I spread her legs and stuck my face into her stench trench. It was like sucking on battery acid. I guess she drank too many of those nasty herbs and they gave her a rotten pussy. After a few stinky seconds, she pulled on my ears, lifting my head up. I needed to sneeze but I held it in.

"Do you have anything?" Her voice was far away.

"Oh, no. I uh . . . Do you?"

"Oh well, I guess it's okay." She ran her nails up and down my bag, which made me tingly and nervous. She pulled me inside her with a sigh and it was like opening a warm grilled cheese sandwich. I pumped and pumped while she squeezed my ass, her nails digging in hard. She kept her eyes closed and I wondered if she was imagining she was somewhere else, with someone else, and if I should be too. I could feel it coming, so I pulled out and gave her a money shot. I'm not sure if she appreciated that or not. She grabbed a shirt beside the bed and wiped me off her face.

"Sorry?"

"No, no, don't worry. I hear it's good for the skin anyway." She giggled and climbed down the ladder to use the bathroom.

I grabbed the glass of water beside the bed and rinsed my mouth and gargled with it, then spit it back into the glass. Then I didn't know what to do, so I flopped back on the mattress and tried to sleep. When she came back she stroked my hair and kissed me on the cheek.

"Happy Valentine's Day, Anthony."

"Yeah, you too," I mumbled. I had forgotten her name. I thought about staying till the morning so she could make me breakfast, but it would be too awkward. Not worth it. I slept for a few hours then snuck out as the sky began to lighten.

The air smelled sweet and the streets were wet and shiny. There was a soft wind blowing the cherry blossoms around like pink confetti. The air was full of them. The gutters were full of them. They floated around my head like scented snowflakes. No one was out. No cars. No buses. No bums. No one. I felt like I was the only person in the city, like the city was a movie set, and I was just passing through it on my way to the real world.

When I got home I had a shower and brushed my teeth. Twice. I smoked a cigarette and waited for the bagel shop to open so I could go see the cute chick who worked there. I drew for a while, sketching out different versions of the tattoo I was going to give myself later that day. Around 8:30, I walked down to get my bagel.

"How's it going?" I asked her.

"Uh, kinda rough today, actually. I went pretty hard last night." She sniffed.

"Oh yeah? I guess Valentine's can do that to you." I laughed.

"Having your usual?"

"Yeah, thanks."

She smeared my everything bagel with cream cheese while I helped myself to coffee, watching her out of the corner of my eye. She had this gorgeous dark brown hair that came down to her ass and fantastic tits which peeked out over the top of her apron. She was short with dimples, and eyes the colour of champagne. Damn, I'd like to fill the hole of that bagel.

"Hey, do you mind if I eat this in here today?"

"Sure." She shrugged. A timer beeped and she went around the corner to take a tray out of the oven. I sat on a stool at the tiny round table beside the window, the only place to sit in the shop. My bagel was hot and delicious and perfect. Probly because she made it.

"So, what are you up to today?"

"Um, selling bagels?"

"Right." Idiot.

"You?" She sniffed.

"Getting a tattoo."

"Oh yeah?" She came out from behind the counter and poured coffee into a pink mug that said: I don't need your attitude, I have my own. She had some flour on her ass and I wanted so badly to dust it off for her.

"Yeah."

"What are you getting?"

"A red ant." I pushed the other stool out with my foot so she would come over and sit down with me. "That's my name, Ant. Or Anthony, if you like."

"I'm Kate, or Kathryn, if you like." She smiled, stuck out her hand. I couldn't tell if she was making fun of me or not. She sat down and we drank our coffees together and no one else came in and it was nice. I could've stayed there with her all day, just sitting there, looking out the window, drinking coffee.

"Where are you gonna get it?"

"In the ditch I think." I studied my forearm.

"I don't know that place. Is it here in Vic?"

"It's what we call this spot right here." I touched the inside of her elbow and it was so soft I got a little shiver.

"Who's we?"

"Tattoo artists."

"You are?"

"I'm apprenticing right now. But eventually I want to open my own shop."

"Is it gonna be life-sized?"

"The shop?"

"The ant."

"No," I laughed. "Probly about the size of two toonies."

"Cool."

Outside, the rain started to ping against the window beside us. My coffee was gone. My bagel was gone. Kate was staring off into the distance.

"Guess I'd better get going. Thanks for the bagel, Kate."

"Yeah, no problem, see ya later. Hey, good luck today."

I don't need luck. I just need a steady hand, I thought, as the bells on the door tinkled behind me.

I never really believed in luck, good or bad. I think things just happen. Some things are good. Some things are bad. Some things are good for some people, but bad for others. There's no reason for any of it, there's no great plan, people live and things happen and then they die and things keep on happening. Luck has nothing to do with it. Luck was probly invented by some asshole who wanted to sell rabbit's feet but couldn't figure out how to get people to buy them.

I headed towards Cook Street and passed a shooting gallery. I looked down the concrete stairwell littered with condoms and syringes and bottles and matches and garbage. I saw seven junkies down there. They looked sick and old and dirty. One of them got up and whistled through her rotten teeth at me. I stopped walking and stared at her. I couldn't help it. I stared. Her hair was colourless and fell to her bare shoulders, her skin was the colour of the sky before it's going to rain, and her eyes, her eyes weren't even human anymore.

"I got what you want, baby," she called up to me. Her voice was raw and scratchy, and I hated her for yelling at me. I wanted to get as far away from her as I could, but her alien eyes held me there. I couldn't move and I couldn't look away. Her eyes were like shards of glass with a pinprick pupil floating in the centre. I wanted to look into her eyes until I had an answer. Until my heart stopped racing. Until something somewhere made sense again. I wanted to tell her she didn't need to be down there. But a part of me knew that she did. There was nowhere else she belonged or would ever belong more than down in that disgusting pit. She tossed her head back and laughed a terrible, soundless laugh, and time started again. I turned away, repulsed. I kept walking.

I walked to the beach at the end of Dallas Road, trying to erase that whole sickening scene. I watched the waves pound into the rocks for a while. There were happy dogs running around with sticks and I thought maybe it would be nice to have a dog one day. A good, smart dog that didn't shed or drool or bark incessantly. I thought about the cougar from last night. Deborah? Brenda? Linda? I hoped I wouldn't run into her around town, but if I did I would pretend not to see her, pretend I didn't know who she was. I'd look right through her. I tried not to think about the junky with the lightning eyes. She made me feel sick and sad and angry. I thought about my ant tattoo. It would be good. It would be great. Right placement. Right design. Bright colour. It would be my first tattoo and it would be perfect.

....

I got to Capital around quarter after four. Hank was twisting up a joint and Sonya was just leaving. I was half relieved and half disappointed that she wouldn't be there to see me execute my first real live tattoo on human flesh. But she made me kinda nervous, so it was probly best that she fucked off.

"You ready for this, kid?" Hank passed me the joint.

"Yeah, better not."

"Right. So get started on your stencil, unless you're gonna freehand it, in which case I'll be really fuckin impressed." He took a long hit on the j and puffed out fat smoke rings that floated above his gleaming head.

I washed my hands at the sink, got out the stencil paper, and carefully drew my ant. Head. Thorax. Abdomen. Two eyes on the side of the head. Two antennae. Six legs. Just like real life, only bigger. I ran the drawing through the Thermofax machine, the way Sonya had shown me, to get my stencil. I would've preferred the ant on my left arm, but since I was gonna be inking it and I'm left handed, it had to be right. I set up my station, set out my ink caps. Black. Red. White. I soaked a makeup pad in alcohol and wiped my inner arm, then I sprayed and washed my arm with the green antibac soap. I got out a razor.

"Gloves!" Hank called from his desk.

"It's my own arm!"

"GLOVES!"

"That's like wearing a condom to masturbate," I mumbled.

"WHAT?"

"I said OKAY." I snapped on a pair. Then I shaved the inside of my forearm, even though there wasn't really any hair there. I threw out the razor and washed again with green soap. I lined up my design and carefully pressed the stencil to the inside of my elbow and rubbed deodorant overtop of it to make it stick. I peeled off the back of the sheet. My fingers were trembling with anticipation. The stencil looked good. It was right and straight. I scooped some Vaseline out of the jar with a tongue depressor and smeared it over the skin I'd be tattooing. I grabbed a wad of paper towels so I'd have them ready when I needed to wipe away the excess ink. Then I ripped the cellophane off a pack of clean tubing that I had sterilized, autoclaved, wrapped, and check-marked a few days ago. I took out the needles. Took out the tube. Put the tube in the tattoo machine. Bagged it. Plugged the electric clip cord into the machine. Pressed the foot pedal. The buzz vibrated through my fingers, through my hand, up my arm, into my brain. I can still hear that buzz now. I dipped the round liner into the little cap of black ink, took a deep breath, and began.

....

It was not painful. It was exhilarating. In, out. In, out. I traced the outline of the ant. Dip. Press. Penetrate. Glide. In. Out. In and out, a thousand times a minute. My hand was steady. My mind was steady. I was completely focused, completely in the present moment. Hank, and the walls, and the world outside melted away. It was only me and my arm and the machine and the ink. Time disappears when I'm tattooing. I can't explain that. It just happens. Little ruby red beads of blood boiled to the surface as I began shading, and I remember thinking, That blood looks so beautiful.

My first tattoo took thirty-three minutes from laying down the stencil to applying the bandage. Hank timed me. I was satisfied with what I'd done. The outline was unbroken, smooth, thick black. The fill was a brilliant red, solid, evenly shaded. There was no blow out or anything and it healed really well, no holidays, just right. I got a kick out of the placement because when I bent my arm, it looked like I was squishing the ant inside my elbow, but when I straightened out again, he recovered. Resilient little bugger.

"Not bad, not too bad," Hank said, clucking his tongue, inspecting the work carefully. "Now give yourself some good advice."

"Uh, don't piss into the wind."

"Try something related to your tattoo, retard." Hank smacked the back of my head.

"Keep it clean. Don't get it wet for a couple weeks. Keep it outta sunlight and pussies. Put only this shit we sell on it. Not Polysporin. Not KY. Not Vaseline. Apply a thin layer of Tattoo Magic morning and night. Don't drown it in the shit. Just a nice thin layer twice a day."

"And?"

"Under no circumstances should I succumb to the temptation to pick the scab."

"Good."

"If I need a touch-up, I can do that no charge."

"Only say that if you want me to kick you in the teeth."

"Oh."

"Touch-ups are almost as annoying as you are, okay? They take up a lot of time and generate zero dinero. Actually, you're gonna do all the touch-ups from now on, what do you say to that?"

"Okay."

"In the old days we could charge for touch-ups and that was a nice bundle of change at the end of the month, but no one charges for maintenance anymore so neither can we. In fact, some guys used to sell tattoo cream to their clients that would help it heal faster but actually fade the colours, so then the poor bastards would have to come back and pay for touch-ups."

"Suckers."

"Okay, Ant-man, get outta my face. And be here bright and early tomorrow."

"Noon?"

"Yep. And Ant, you're pushing ink tomorrow. Bring your A-game."

My arm was hot and stung like I'd been burned. I practically floated out the door. I could hear the buzz of the tattoo machine humming in my ears all the way home.

....

That night I went to bed early. I dreamt of the junky with the lightning eyes. She was picking at my skin, scratching me, poking me. I didn't want her to touch my tattoo. I didn't want her to get it infected. I didn't want her to touch me at all, anywhere. Her mouth was moving like she was talking, but I couldn't hear anything she said. I knew she was trying to tell me something important, but I couldn't hear her. I kept asking her: "What are you saying? What? Pardon? Repeat yourself."

And her mouth just kept moving and moving like one of those wooden puppets, and her eyes were so bright and cold. I grabbed her by the shoulders and shook her. "What are you trying to tell me?" I yelled into her face. I shook her and shook her until she crumbled into little pieces at my feet. Like little pieces of glass. I tried to scoop up the shards and put her back together, but I cut my hands and arms and they were gushing blood everywhere and my tattoo was cut and ruined.

I woke up wringing my pillow, every muscle rigid. I got up and poured a drink of water. I smoked a pinner. Then I drew for a while. I drew her, even though I didn't want to. I didn't get her right and I didn't care. I never wanted to see her again.

············

The next day was dead slow. Sonya left early. I cleaned everything in the shop. I cleaned all the machines and stencils and ran everything through the autoclave. I cleaned the front window inside and out and polished the chrome counter. I dusted the sheets of flash on the walls, wiped down the chairs, and swept and mopped the floor. I even washed out the jar Hank kept his pencil crayons in. Only four people came in all day. Two of them looked around for a while, then left. One of them wanted to know where the mall was. One of them was a touch-up: a chick with a dolphin on her ankle. Her ankles were fat and so was she. It took me five minutes to blue up that little fish. The ink flowed in smoothly and it was almost easier than doing a grapefruit, except grapefruits don't talk and giggle and try to flirt with you.

"Go lock the door," Hank said when she left. "We're closed." He sighed, took out his bag of bud. "Days like that make me nervous, know what I mean?"

"Yeah."

"You got plans tonight, kid?"

"Not really."

"You do now. I'm takin you out."

"Oh yeah, where we goin?"

"Fight club. Meet me here at eight."

"As long as I don't have to fight."

Hank laughed. "You won't."

I nodded and left without taking a hoot. The sun was shining and I wanted to get the hell out of there. I stopped by the bagel shop on my way home. Kate was closing up for the day. She had a big bag of day old bagels that she was gonna throw out, but I intercepted her at the dumpster and got breakfast, lunch, and dinner for the next couple days.

"Hey, let's see your tattoo," she said.

I pulled up my sleeve obediently.

"Wow. You did that?" Her eyes shone golden in the sunlight.

"Yeah."

"Did it hurt?"

"No."

"That's so great." She looked like she wanted to touch it, but didn't dare. Two bike couriers whizzed by, one was on a fixie and he was doing some wicked manoeuvre, standing up, with his arms outstretched, leaning out over his handle bars, Titanic style. But Kate didn't take her eyes off my ant.

Out there in the parking lot that afternoon, standing beside a dumpster, holding a bag of bagels, I felt the power of a tattoo. It was like a cross between a magnet and a talisman.

"Do you have a smoke I could borrow?" she asked, looking at my pockets.

"Yeah, sure." I gave her a cigarette and lit it for her, holding her eyes with mine.

"Thanks."

"No problem." We stood there for a while, smoking, not saying anything, letting the sun warm our faces.

"Do you like coke?"

"I don't have any of that."

"Yeah, but do you like it?"

"Sometimes."

"How bout now?" She raised her eyebrow, then turned and trotted towards the door. I watched her ass for a few seconds. Ah, what the hell? I thought, and followed her inside.

She flicked on the radio and led me to the back kitchen and laid two fat rails out on the stainless steel countertop. We snorted them up through green plastic straws. I could see my wide-face funhouse reflection in the counter as I leaned over it. "Free Fallin'" came on the radio and Kate sang along with Tom Petty. She had a real nice singing voice. It had been awhile since I'd had coke, not since I left Calgary. It occurred to me then that I had missed it. I got a head rush and my nose burned and my clothes felt itchy. I wanted to grab Kate and throw her onto the counter and fuck her right then and there. But her cellphone rang. She answered it and turned away to talk in a quiet, worried voice. She hung up after a minute or five and turned to me.

"You gotta go," she said. "That was my boyfriend."

No, dammit. No. This can't be right. She'd used the b-word. This was not what I'd envisioned. I looked at the countertop longingly. She was not on it, naked and panting. This was all wrong.

"Please go now, Ant." A tiny trickle of blood oozed from her left nostril and it turned my stomach.

"No problem. See ya later." I pushed through the back emergency exit out into the too-bright sunlight of the parking lot. Two bums were picking through the dumpster. When they saw me with the bag of bagels in my hand they let the lid fall and ambled away.

I went back to my room at the George & Dragon. It smelled like stale beer and onion rings. I had a super hot shower and then jerked off for a while, thinking of Kate, and then Sonya, and then Kate and Sonya together, and then me and Sonya and Kate. Then Hank's head popped into my head and that was bad, and then I realized it was almost eight and I had to go meet him.

....

I had a smoke outside of Capital Tattoo while I waited for Hank. I heard him before I saw him. The rumble. He roared up on his Harley about quarter after eight and tossed me a helmet. I pulled it over my head and climbed on behind him. We zoomed through the cool night, city lights bowing before us. I opened the shield on my helmet so I could feel the air hit my face, held onto the backrest so I didn't have to wrap my arms around Hank. He drove to the industrial part of town and pulled in behind an ugly, unmarked grey warehouse with a bunch of other bikes and cars and trucks in the parking lot. We went to the back door and a huge hulk of a man stood in front of it.

"Who the fuck are you?" He stepped towards me.

"It's okay, Donnie, he's with me," Hank said.

He looked at Hank like he wanted to squash him. He scowled at me.

"He's cool. Don't worry."

"I gotta search both of you," he growled.

I put my arms out while the guy patted me down, tried not to flinch when he ran his paws over my crotch. He glared at us and opened the door. I let Hank lead the way, down some concrete steps to a big dark basement full of men and dogs.

....

There were about thirty men and I could see six dogs. It smelled like sweat and blood and dog piss. I felt my jaw clench tight and my hands turn clammy. I wished I had another line. I wished I had a beer. I wasn't ready for this.

A guy with a scar through his eyebrow was yelling, "Place your bets! Place your bets, boys!" and walking around with a black box collecting money.

"Got any dough?" Hank asked.

"Sure don't."

"Here," he handed me a fifty. "That's a loan."

The next fight was between a white beast of a dog that was about the size of a shopping cart. Pure muscle, eh. This thing was hardly even recognizable as a dog, he was an APBT machine, and he was gonna be fighting this little tan pit bull that looked like she was new to the ring. The owners were getting them all riled up in their corners of the box.

"Who're you betting on?" Hank yelled into my ear.

"The tan one."

"That little shitbitch? She's gonna get eaten!"

"It's not the size of the dog in the fight, Hank. It's the size of the fight in the dog." Seth used to say that when I was a kid and I'd come home from school all bloodied up from a fight. I didn't really understand what he meant back then, but for some reason, it always made me feel better.

Hank grinned crazily at me. "I can't tell if you're really stupid, or you just pretend to be sometimes."

"Me neither," I said.

The ref counted down from thirty and the dogs were let off their chains. They scrapped around and snarled for a few seconds, then the little tan pit bull got a lock on the white beast's snout. She was locked on for a few minutes. I could feel my heart banging inside my head. There were shouts in the crowd. Clouds of smoke hovered above us. The white dog flipped over and shook the other dog off. Then he lunged at her front leg and chomped down, but the little tan pit bull went for the white dog's face again. I was partly disgusted and partly fascinated. The dogs circled the box, locked onto each other for what seemed like hours. Sweat dripped down the back of my neck. I lit a cigarette. My mouth was so dry.

Time slows right down during a dog fight. It's amazing how quiet the dogs are. They're getting torn apart, but they hardly make a sound.

The ref called the match after the little tan pit bull had the white beast on the ground in a throat hold for a few minutes. The white dog's legs were still, he had stopped fighting back. He had an eye socket ripped out, one ear in shreds, and his face was just a bloody mess of ground dog meat. The little tan pit bull was bleeding and falling all over the place, but she was named champion. Baby, was her name. I remember that. Hank clapped me on the back and I swallowed a little bit of puke that had snuck up my throat. I left with $300 in my pocket.

....

I went to the dog fights every week for a few months and, for a while, I was considering getting in on some of the action. Start bringing in some serious cash for once. You know, get some dogs, train em up, put em in the ring. How hard could it be? The dogs do the hard part. Some of those goddamn dogs are worth twenty-five, thirty grand, even more once they've won a few important fights. So I started looking up some guys who maybe knew where I could get some American pit bull terrier puppies. I learned if you wanna go pro, you can't just get any pit puppy, you gotta research the bloodlines and get the offspring of a champion fighter, then you gotta pour a whole bunch of money into that dog, get all its training equipment, treadmills and jumps and weights and shit, feed it top of the line food to turn it into pure muscle, and then invest in a bunch of drugs and surgical tools so you can fix it up after fights. I'd have to move somewheres with a yard and some privacy. And then the dog could just fall down and die its first night in the ring after I went and blew all that money on it. Well, it seemed like more of a pain in the ass at that point, kinda a high risk investment, if you know what I mean, and I didn't have the capital to start up then anyways.

Grace used to say, "If you're good at something, stick with it." So that's what I decided to do with tattooing. Like I said, drawing's probly the only thing I was ever any good at. But the dog fights were good for keeping me in smokes and what have you. On a few occasions, I was only able to eat that night because I'd picked the right dog. And by that point I was really, really sick and tired of never having any money. They had cut me down to three nights a week at the George, which was barely enough to survive on. Hank was true to his word, he never paid me a cent for an entire year of work. And, yes, I had to do some of the nastiest tatts in the west.

....

It blew my mind some of the hideous shit people wanted on their bodies. Forever. I tattooed some real fucking ugly fucking tacky ass shit on some nice-looking people. Some of the stuff I tattooed, I'm really ashamed of. I did tattoos I knew people would regret for the rest of

their lives. I have made perfect flesh grotesque. It's scarring someone
for life, you know, really. And they'll always remember it was me who
did it to them. But I can't take responsibility for other people's actions,
people are allowed to make their own choices, you know? Yeah, your
tattoo is a fuckin joke, but so are you, so, whatever.

Call me traditional, but I think a ripped up zombie bride with
pieces of her own green, bloody face falling off and her tongue sticking
out like she wants to lick you or eat her own face or both, is a little
distasteful to want covering your entire arm. At least put it on your
ass or something, so other people won't have to look at it. And the
Tasmanian Devil jerking off? Who would want to look down at their
body and see that on themselves every day? But I did it. I did it. I did
that and much worse. So many maple leafs, so many butterflies, so
many Yosemite Sams. I hated doing cartoon characters, and I hated
Yosemite Sam the most. I wanted to knock the teeth out of every idiot
who asked for one. I swore once I stopped apprenticing with Hank, I
would never make a Yosemite Sam tattoo ever, ever again. Maybe even
worse than Yosemite Sam was Winnie the Pooh. Imagine marking
someone for life with Winnie the fucking Pooh. It was a terrible feeling.
He is not cute. He is not funny. He is stupid. Stupid. Stupid. Stupid.
I can pretty much guarantee you that anyone asking for a Winnie the
Pooh tattoo is mentally unstable, if not completely fuckin retarded.
Winnie's yellow, right, and yellow ink doesn't stay in that well, so I
usually had to see every Winnie two or three more times for touch-
ups. I hated myself when I was tattooing Winnie the Pooh.

I also hated: sports team names, gang names, lover's names,
and bands. Don't these people ever think they'll change their mind?
Jesus. I also hated doing portraiture. I don't care how good of a tattooist
you are, or you think you are, portraits, people's cheesy-looking faces,
never look good. Even if you got someone rad, like Jim Morrison or
Hendrix, it would still look crappy, let alone someone normal, like
your stupid kid or your ugly wife or your dorky parents. It just doesn't
work as a tattoo. That's what photographs are for.

I remember this one awful week at the shop, after I'd been
tattooing about four months, this real pretty chick came in, she was
probly eighteen or nineteen, blonde, great body. What does she want?

She wants the name of her frigging loser boyfriend, Godfrey, in OE Script across her left breast. Unreal. Oh man, she had these perfect, luscious breasts too. I hated Godfrey. Whoever he was, he did not deserve this. I tried to talk her out of it, the way Sonya would have. I suggested alternate placement, I suggested taking more time to think about it, but she was determined. There was no chance of me changing her mind, and Hank was watching. I wished Sonya had been there to use her Super Shadow powers of persuasion. But she had gone to a tattoo convention in Vancouver.

"How long have you been together?" I asked as I carefully soaped her up.

"Almost five months."

"Are you one hundred percent sure that you want this tattoo here forever?"

"Listen," she leaned towards me, lowered her voice, "we almost broke up yesterday. I think this is really going to save us." She smiled, her green eyes filled with tears.

As I set up the stencil I stared hard at Hank, silently begging him not to make me do this, to save this girl from certain cruelty. But Hank just made a lewd gesture with his tongue and then went to the can. If Hank hadn't been there, I would have sent her away toot sweet. But this is what I'd signed up for, this is what I'd agreed to do. God, I hated to mar her perfect breast like that. Especially since cum guzzling Godfrey would probly dump her in a few weeks anyway. It was torture. I felt sick, carving that name into her. It was painful. I had no right to do that to her. No right at all.

"I love it!" she chirped when it was over.

I wonder if she still does.

....

I left early that day. Told Hank I wasn't feeling well, which was true. Went home and took so many bong hits I couldn't see anymore. Then I flopped down on my bed and spanked it so hard for so long that my dick got these sore little cuts all over it and I had to stop. I passed out and dreamt about sucking that chick's clean, perfect breast, but then her nipple turned into a gun barrel and I grabbed her other breast, which was the trigger, and the gun went off in my mouth and blew a hole through the back of my head.

....

The day after that wasn't so shithot either. Sonya was back, which was good, but she wouldn't share anything she'd seen at the tattoo expo, which was bad. Really bad. Because I was pretty sure she'd seen a sweet suspension and I wanted to hear all about it. But what did I get? Nothing. It was like ripping out teeth, trying to get anything out of that woman. Tight lips. Well, better tight than loose, I always say.

Sonya was very competitive and, even though I was only a lowly apprentice then, I guess she didn't want me to be competition for her later on.

Just after noon, these two beefy jock chumps came in. No surprise, they want red maple leafs on their shoulders. Okay, simple enough. No big deal, right? So I do the first guy, takes about twenty minutes, he's happy, he's stoked on his tacky maple leaf. His buddy kept asking him the whole time, "Does it hurt? Does it hurt?" Which was so irritating, I almost slapped him. And then it's buddy's turn and this is his first tattoo and he's kinda pale. As I applied the stencil I noticed his skin was clammy and beads of sweat were collecting around his lips. I figured he was just nervous and didn't think much of it. The first needle in, he flinched. I stopped the machine.

"You can't move, okay?"

"Sorry. Okay. Sorry, sorry." He swallowed.

About two minutes later I looked up to see how he's doing, and his fuckin eyeballs are rolled back in his head. Then he started convulsing and I pulled the machine away just before he puked all over me. He kept puking and puking all over the chair and the floor and himself, and then he pissed his pants.

"What the fuck is this?" I turned to his friend.

"Dan, Dan! Are you okay? It's alright, man, just take it easy."

Dan kept puking and shaking and started shitting right there in the chair.

"Hank! I need you out here!" I yelled. "Now!"

Hank stepped out from the back room. "Oh shit," he said, and picked up the phone to call 911. Sonya walked in the door then with our morning coffees and croissants. "Oh shit," she said. She looked at me, splashed in vomit, and a smirk flickered across her face. She shook her head and set down the coffees, covered her mouth with her hand. I could tell by her eyes, she was laughing. Dan was on his hands and knees on the floor, still throwing up. A puddle of piss dripped off the chair and there were brown stains seeping through his jeans. It smelled like the nastiest fuckin shit ever laid. I knew I would puke if I kept watching him so I went to the can and took off my shirt and washed up as best as I could in the sink. I gagged a little bit. All I could smell was puke and shit. It was disgusting. I figured Dan was gonna die and that I'd be held responsible for his death. Maybe I hadn't sterilized something properly, or maybe he was allergic to the ink or the metal or something. I figured he would probly already be dead when I came out of the bathroom.

But he wasn't.

He was moaning and rocking back and forth in a pathetic mess on the floor, and the four of us looked on while we waited for the ambulance to get there. They took fuckin forever to get there. Hank turned the sign over so no one else would come in. Sonya handed me my coffee: "No point letting it get cold." I took it from her, but I could only take a few small sips. I put both hands around the cup, the heat somehow a comfort. After that no one said anything. Slayer played on the stereo. Hank lit a cigarette. A heavy rain drummed against the roof. We waited. I wanted them to hurry up and get there and take him away. If Dan died, I wanted him to die in the hospital and not in Hank's shop. Finally, they came. I suddenly felt very, very tired and wanted to lie down on a stretcher too. But Hank shoved a mop into my hand and clapped real loud in front of my face. I had to clean it all up. Sonya and Hank could barely control their laughter.

"I guess I should've warned you," Hank said, chuckling. "About four people in a hundred get sick. It's mostly nerves."

"Oh, shit."

"I guess this is your lucky day."

....

I skated home after that with no shirt on, and the rain splattered against my chest and back, and it was cold and sharp and good. I talked Carmen into giving me free tea and toast. She asked me if I was sick and I said yes and she put her hand on my forehead, and her hand was so soft and cool I thought I might like her to keep it there for a while. But she pulled it away and said, "You don't have a fever."

"Thank you." I took the toast and tea up to my room and listened to the radio for a while, trying to erase the day from my mind. There was a sexy sounding DJ on the campus station and she was playing some pretty trippy tunes. Some Frank Zappa. Some Lou Reed. The music she played cheered me up a little, and I thought about calling her up and requesting a song or something. But I couldn't think of anything I wanted to hear. And I couldn't think of anything to say to her, except, "I think you have a sexy voice." So I didn't call.

....

The next day it was just me and Sonya working. Hank had to go to some conference in Nanaimo. It was my first time working alone with Sonya. I must've thought about jumping her bones about ten thousand times that day. I smoked an entire pack of cigarettes. It was slow, and Sonya spent most of her time drawing, sitting at Hank's desk. I badly wanted to see what she was doing, but I didn't ask her if I could see it, I didn't go look over her shoulder. I sort of liked imagining what she was drawing. And I couldn't help imagining that Sonya was naked behind that desk. She was wearing a strapless shirt what do they call those? Tube tops or something. That shirt was really unfair. That day was the first time at Capital Tattoo that I had to go into the can and jerk off. I had to. It was the only way I would've been able to get through the entire day without going insane.

In the late afternoon this gangly lookin kid with fat dreads came in. Sonya was talking to him when I came out of the can.

"I want a facial tattoo, you know, like the New Zealand natives, just here." He pushed his dirty pink finger into his chin.

"You want a moko?"

"Yeah, that's what they're called."

"Are you Maori?"

"No."

"Have you ever been to New Zealand?"

"No, man, I just think they look fuckin cool."

I tried to stay quiet at the back of the room where I was wiping the mirrors, and I had to smother a little laugh.

"So, let me get this straight," Sonya said. "You want to wear this traditional tattoo from a culture you know nothing about, on your face, for the whole world to see, for the rest of your life, because you think it looks fuckin cool?"

"Yeah, that's about it." He smacked his gum around in his mouth.

"Well, you're gonna have to find someone else to do that for you then, cause I'm sure as fuck not."

"Why not?" The kid looked to me for help, his ugly little face screwed up in confusion. "I'm the customer. The customer's always right."

"Yeah? You can get right out of this shop."

"What's your problem, man? Hey, what's her problem?" he called over to me. "I thought this was a tattoo parlour. You're telling me I can't get the tattoo I want? What the fuck is that?"

"You better just go, man," I said, nodding my head towards the door.

Sonya got up and walked into the back room, closed the door with a click.

"Fine, I'll take my business elsewhere," he yelled, and stormed out, slamming the door behind him.

I went into the back. Sonya was drinking a tall glass of water. "You okay?"

She shrugged, swallowed. "I just can't do what I know isn't right, you know?"

"Yeah," I said. "You're good."

....

A few weeks after the shittymaplepukeleaf incident, I had another tattoo nightmare come true. I'd been hoping all along that this wouldn't happen, at least not while I was apprenticing under Hank, but then, one day, it did.

A guy wanted me to tattoo his dick. He was short with humongous arms and no neck. He was probly on steroids or something. I asked him if he was sure and he said he was absolutely sure. I asked him if he wanted to think about it for a few days and make an appointment to come back. Nope. He was sure. He wanted it today. Now. He had wanted it for a long time and he wasn't going to change his mind. What did he want? He wanted black tiger stripes encircling his schlong.

I could either run out the door and never come back, or do it. I went into the back room for a minute to think about what I would do. I drank a big glass of water without breathing. I wanted to run. But I wanted to finish my apprenticeship. And a part of me sort of wanted to see if the guy would actually go through with it. I wanted to call his bluff. Hank was there, so I couldn't say no. Fuck, I wanted to though. I never wanted to be in a situation where I had to hold another guy's cock in my hand. But here I was and, the worst part was, I wasn't even gonna get paid for it. I walked back out into the main room. Hank and Sonya were laughing behind their hands at me the whole time and I hated them both.

"Okay, let's get started," I said. I took him into the private room and gave Hank and Sonya the finger before I closed the door.

I could tell the guy was nervous as fuck when he undid his pants. He fumbled with his belt and zipper like an anxious virgin. I just hoped I wouldn't see a repeat of the maple leaf episode. I set up my station and told him to sit down, relax, and take some deep breaths. I told him we could take a break at any time and to just let me know whenever he needed to stop because this was probly gonna sting a little. He nodded and took out his dink and it flopped on the chair like a slug. It was short and fat and ugly as sin. The big purple vein running through the centre looked evil and menacing. I stared at it and it stared right back up at me. An acrid, nasty taste welled up in my throat. I turned away from him and spat into the garbage can.

ashley little

43

prick

I don't understand how women could want these repulsive things inside them. All of a sudden, I felt sorry for women. Straight women, that is. Not dykes. Dykes got it figured out. I snapped on a pair of gloves and looked at Tony the Tiger. He had gone pale as a maggot.

"You alright?"

"Yeah." He swallowed.

I sprayed some soap on him and started to wipe it. He flinched and jumped back a little. I guess I would have too if some dude was touching my member. But I laughed at him anyway. "Are you gonna be doing that when I have the tattoo machine in my hand?"

"Sorry. I, uh, I guess I should go to the washroom first."

"Good idea."

He left the room and I put my head down and laughed silently. I could hardly believe I was going to do what I was about to do. When he walked back in I covered my laughing by pretending to cough. He sat down and took himself out again.

"Why don't you tell me about your stripes, how thick you want em and that."

Once he got talking he calmed down a little. I had a hell of a hard time shaving him though. I don't know if you've ever shaved a flaccid penis before, but let me tell you, it is no easy task. Finally, I was ready to roll. "Alright, dude, this is your last chance to change your mind. No one will blame you if you do."

He closed his eyes and leaned back in his chair and let out a long, loud breath through his mouth. He clenched and unclenched his hands. He scratched his head with both hands and then his eyes popped open. "I'm ready," he said. "Let's do it."

I started up my machine and stretched the rubbery skin of his penis. I began to tattoo his stripes.

It bled a fuck of a lot, which I was sort of expecting. Thank God he had his eyes closed most of the time so he couldn't see how much he was bleeding. After a few minutes of concentrating, I sort of forgot I was tattooing a penis. It was just like tattooing any other part of the body, except that it was more private. The guy was doing pretty well. I kept asking him if he needed a break and he'd say, "No. Keep going. Don't stop now." Sometimes he would grit his teeth together or claw into the arms of the chair, but I had to admire his endurance. He never got hard, thank fuck. Maybe he had some sort of dysfunction and he thought the tiger stripes would help heal him, I don't know. But I was glad for it. I don't know what I would've done if he'd gotten hard. It took about thirty-five minutes to give him the stripes he wanted, and I have to say, he earned em.

....

I remember the first time I saw a penis that wasn't my own. Seth's. I walked into the bathroom one morning while he was getting ready for work. I was probly four or five or something. It scared me. It was so huge and dangling right in my face. I must've looked scared, cause he laughed at me. And his penis shook when he laughed. He told me I would have a big one too one day, and that I could squirt it just like a water gun.

"Really?"

"No, kid, I'm lying to you."

"Oh."

I never knew what to believe from Seth's mouth. Grace always said he made his living lying. He was a used car salesman.

....

My next big tattoo challenge came in soon after Tony the Tiger. It was a custom demon scene on this guy's back. It was a major piece of work. It took almost twenty-four hours to complete. In different sittings, obviously. It turned out pretty killer, and is one of my favourite tattoos that I've done. I was gaining more confidence in my ability to shade and freehand, which I figure is the mark of a real artist. Any idiot can trace a stencil. But to design and draw your own skin pictures is something completely different. I think Hank was pleased with my work as well, which, I'll admit, felt good. When I had finished the last session on demon guy, Sonya and Hank came over to inspect it.

"Keep doin work like this and you'll have the skin peeler after your clients." Hank laughed.

Sonya shook her head and rolled her eyes.

"What's that?" Demon guy asked.

"He's sick, don't listen to him," Sonya said.

"The skin peeler collects tattoos," Hank said.

"Yeah?"

"Other people's tattoos."

"Oh." He looked at his back in the mirror, his face knotted with concern. "Ew."

"But don't worry, he hasn't made a big peel here in a couple years now. We think he's moved over to the mainland."

The guy thanked me and paid, his eyes nearly popping out of his head. The wind sucked the door closed behind him with a bang. Hank chuckled to himself behind his desk as he lit a smoke.

"That was mean," Sonya said.

"Aw, come on, I was just havin some fun with him."

"You are one sick puppy, Hank."

"Listen, kids, monsters only come for you if you leave your cellar door open."

....

Eventually, I completed a big piece on my lower left leg that was a very similar demonic scene, done all in fine line black and grey. It looked wicked. Still does. It's one of my favourites, even though I prefer to work with vibrant colours now.

When we smoked a joint at closing time that afternoon, Hank said, "You're coming to a party tonight."

"I am?"

"Yup."

"What kinda party?"

"The best kind there is."

"Which is?"

"A Lucifer's Choice party."

"Oh Jesus." I had figured that Hank was a member of the LC motorcycle gang through slices of conversation and things I'd seen. I didn't know how high up he was, if he was a full patch or a prez or

what. I know he tattooed a lotta them. I know he was highly respected.
I think he tried to keep a low pro on his status because he wanted
Capital to be a legit business and didn't want it coming under scrutiny
or getting shut down. He didn't wear his colours or have any gang
paraphernalia at work. I guess he was like an undercover member.

"I'll pick you up at your place at eight."

I hesitated. But then I figured, I got nothing to lose. "Alright,"
I said. "Like my old man used to say, 'I'm here for a good time, not a
long time.' "

"You won't be sorry, kid."

....

Hank pulled up in front of the George & Dragon around 8:30. Another
guy rode with us. Hank introduced him as Jonesy. He was a wiry,
mean-looking guy with a grey face and a grey beard. He looked like
he'd been living hard and riding hard for a long, long time. They both
had their Lucifer's Choice jackets on. This is gonna be an interesting
night, I thought, and held fast to the back of my seat, adjusted to the
deafening roar of the bikes blocking out all other sounds. I kept taking
huge gulps of air because suddenly the air felt thin and quick and I
couldn't get enough of it. I opened the shield on my helmet. I loved the
feeling of the wind hitting my face, the dizzying rush of the pavement
beneath my feet.

We rode to a clubhouse in Sooke, arriving just as it was getting
too dark to see. There were tons of people inside already and the place
was plush. There were a few biker chicks and some skanky lookin
chicks, and a few hot ass chicks around too. Some cracked out blonde
latched on to Jonesy and they disappeared upstairs. I did a couple nice
lines with Hank and we had a few beers. He introduced me to some
of his buddies. They were all pretty intense dudes. Dudes that you
wouldn't even want to dream about fucking with. Dudes that would
probly smash your kneecaps if you looked at them the wrong way.
Hank knew a lotta people there, I only knew Hank. I lost him after
awhile, and decided to explore on my own. I found a room upstairs
with a soft orange light glowing under the door. I opened the door.

There were two chicks lying on the bed. They both had their shirts off. There were three dudes in there, standing around the bed. They were fully dressed.

"Come in here. Close the door," the biggest guy said.

I closed the door. The chicks looked at me and smiled with their mouths closed. The dudes looked coked to the gills.

"Wanna do a speedball?"

"Sure." I walked over to the bed.

He laid out a rail across the hottest chick's left breast. I thought I'd died and gone to heaven. I took a twenty out of my pocket and rolled it up. I practically jizzed my pants leaning over her to do it. It was all I could do not to put her breast in my mouth. I clamped my lips shut and snorted the line up quick and stood up and my head rushed and my eyes burned and then everything was fine again. Better than fine. I felt a warm glow crawl up the back of my neck and into my brain. After I took my line, everyone else did one, and then I took another little bump and left the room. They didn't even ask me my name or anything. But they got me ridiculously high.

I walked around for a while in a floaty sort of a trance. I found the smoking room. It was all men in there. Lotsa cigars. I had a few puffs off someone's Cohiba and then wandered down to the basement. There was a lotta noise coming from behind a steel door. I opened the door. I saw a circle of men standing around a big cement room, probly about twenty-five, thirty of em. In the middle was a young blonde chick being fucked from behind over a table. Her wrists were tied to the table with rope. I looked in her eyes, and I still wish I hadn't. Her makeup was running all over her face in these little black rivers. She was clearly in pain. It was pretty obvious that she didn't want to be doing what she was doing. She cried out and the guy who was giving it to her slapped her ass with a hard WHACK and the men cheered and whistled and hollered. Her eyes were begging me to help her, to get her out of there. To make her safe. She kept looking at me and looking at me and asking me to help her with her eyes, and I did nothing. I couldn't. I couldn't do a goddamned thing. I looked at the man behind her. It was Hank. Our eyes locked as he thrust himself in and in and into her. And then he came and I turned away and slipped out the door and up the stairs and shoved my way through the crowded hallway and into the foyer full of boots and coats and helmets and purses and out the front door.

....

I walked to the road and threw up in the street. I walked away from the clubhouse. I didn't know which direction I was going or where I was heading, I just knew I was going away from there. I walked as fast as I could. Don't run. Don't run. Don't you dare start fuckin running. But I wanted to.

I kept looking behind me to see who was coming after me. I was really high and tripping out on what I'd just seen. I figured I was gonna get my ass beat, or worse, for leaving that room without taking a turn, but no one was following me. No one was coming. No one had a gun to my head, but I could almost feel the cold muzzle at the base of my skull. Maybe no one had seen me in there except the girl and Hank. I had stood silently in the shadows, and was allowed to leave.

....

I ended up hitching a ride back to Victoria with a Queerbec trucker. He was a pervert, but I didn't let him do anything. He asked me if I would suck him off and I said no fuckin way. He said fine and pulled out a crack pipe and took a hit. He handed me the pipe but I shook my head. I just wanted to get home alive. I figured I would be able to jump out of the truck and roll onto the shoulder if I had to.

I've jumped out of a car before, when I was fourteen. It wasn't too bad. I got a few scrapes, but it wasn't as hard as you'd think it would be. Seth was driving and I was sitting shotgun. He was mad about something, I don't even remember what, and he started hitting me, smacking my head real hard, then he picked up this ceramic coffee mug from the cup holder and started smashing it into the side of my head and my ear. I felt the hot blood ooze out of my ear, and my ear was ringing like a church bell. I couldn't even hear him going on anymore because my ear was ringing so loud. I was like, Fuck this, I'm outta here. I pulled the door handle, covered my head, and jumped, rolled right into the ditch. He didn't stop or turn around or anything, he just kept driving. I didn't go home that night. I slept inside a yellow covered slide in a kiddie park. It was April. It was cold. The next day I saw Seth and he acted like nothing had happened. He didn't say "Sorry" or "How's your ear?" or anything. Just went about his normal routine. But that's just how he was. Never thought he did anything wrong. Never thought he actually hurt you. Or maybe he knew but he just didn't care.

I never told Grace about that time. Because I knew she'd be mad that I jumped out of the car. I still get ringing in that ear sometimes. But it doesn't bother me as much as it used to.

....

Finally, the trucker let me out on Douglas and I walked back to Fernwood. When I got home I threw up again, then I crawled into bed and slept through the rest of the night.

At noon I called Capital Tattoo and my heart was hammering so loud in my head, I was nervous that Hank would be able to hear it through the phone.

"What the fuck happened to you last night?" Hank barked.

"I, uh, I had some business to take care of."

"Is that so?"

"Yeah, had a lady waiting in the wings for me. Didn't want to disappoint her, you know how it is."

"Thatta boy."

"Thing is, I'm not feeling too great today, I think she gave me the flu or something."

"You'll be lucky if that's all she gave you."

"Yeah, so I won't be coming in today."

"Alright, well, you get well soon, kiddo. And Ant?"

"Yeah?"

"I trust you."

"Thanks."

"You get me?"

"Yeah, I get you."

"Good." He hung up.

I didn't go into Capital for the rest of the week. I felt like shit and I couldn't stand to see Hank. The scene in that basement kept replaying itself in my head, even though I didn't want it to. I never wanted to think about it again. I wanted to forget all about it. But there it was, every time I closed my eyes. Fuck, I felt guilty about not helping that girl. Sometimes, when I close my eyes, I can still see her face. Her eyes full of terror and pain, crying those black tears. Eyes that burn holes through your heart.

....

I laid low for a while, worked my dishwashing shifts at the George and got my free meals. The dish pit was a private little corner and no one really came in there to bother me. It was just me and the dishes and the dishwasher and the hose, and it was peaceful and warm and easy.

I called Grace. She wasn't home. I tried calling again. Seth answered. I almost hung up.

"Who's this?" he said.

"It's Anthony."

"An-tony?" He never pronounced the h in my name. It's like he thought I should have a different name. One with no th sound.

"How's it going?"

"Fine."

"Good."

"Yup."

"Is Grace there?"

"No. She's out."

"Oh?"

"Do you need money?"

"Why? Are you sending me some?"

"Goddamn right I'm not. Why are you calling?"

"To say hello?"

"Horseshit."

"Okay, bye Seth."

"Who is this again? Who's calling me at this unholy hour?"

I hung up.

For a long time growing up, I thought it was normal for a guy to hit his wife and grandkid and get drunk every night and yell and smash around the house and sometimes threaten to kill you and your grandma and that was just the way a family worked. Violence and drama around every corner. "Keeps things interesting," Grace used to say. I remember he set her hair on fire when I was six years old. I thought it was a great big joke. I remember laughing. Laughing along with him. Grace ran to the bathroom and stuck her head in the toilet, and we laughed even harder.

I wondered if Grace was out or out. I hated to think that she might be hurt and there was fuck all I could do about it. Not that I ever did anything about it when I lived there. I can't remember ever really standing up to him. I guess I never did. All I did was leave.

....

That night I dreamt I was in the ring with four pit bulls. I was on the ground and they were attacking me, tearing me apart. Limb from fucking limb. I was trying to crawl away, to get up, to kick them in the face, but I couldn't move. I couldn't scream. I couldn't do anything. One ripped off my left leg and ran away with it. Then one ripped off my right leg and started devouring it. Another one tore off my right arm and shook it around, like dogs do. I tried to fight off the last one coming for my left arm, I poked it in the eye, but then it lunged for my face instead. I saw its huge jaws full of ice-pick teeth coming down at me.

Then I woke up, panting.

....

Around this time Sonya finally agreed to give me the tattoo I wanted: a phoenix on my upper back, wings wrapping around my shoulders. It was a big job and took three sittings of about three hours each. We were all alone in the shop each time. It was wonderful. Sonya was different when she was tattooing, she actually talked. With the machine in her hand she would open up. I casually asked her what she thought of Hank being a Lucifer's Choice.

"So what? Who cares?"

"You should care, Sonya."

"Why?"

"Do you have any idea what these guys are capable of?"

"Hey, man, I lived and worked in NYC for two years."

"So?"

"So I know some Wiseguys, okay. Those guys are the real deal and they don't give a flying fuck about Lucifer's Choice. Lucifer's Choice are not even on their radar. I was in Japan last year, okay. I got to witness a master tattoo a Yakuza. LC are a fuckin joke compared to those guys. Believe me."

"No shit, eh?"

"Lucifer's Choice are just a bunch of middle-aged dudes who like to ride motorcycles. I don't get why everyone thinks that's so badass."

I asked her if we could take a smoke break. I wanted a drink. I wanted to take a piss. She'd been working on me for almost two hours. Sonya said no sweat and went out to grab a coffee. I went to the can. I knew they wouldn't touch her, but still, I worried about her. I figured she was protected because of her association with Hank, but maybe she was more vulnerable because of it. I would have to watch out for her.

When she got back she had brought me a coffee and a lemon Danish, and I knew then for sure that I loved her and always would. After I ate and had a cigarette, she started working on me again.

"My dad had a phoenix, on his chest," she said.

"Oh yeah, where's he at?"

"I don't know. I haven't seen him in about twenty years."

"Are you in contact?"

"He used to send postcards every year on my birthday, then every other year, then every fifth year. Eventually they stopped coming."

"What about your mom?"

"She's in Toronto."

"That's where you grew up?"

"Yep."

This phoenix was the biggest piece I'd gotten and it was really intricate but, somehow, with Sonya holding the machine, it didn't hurt. It felt incredible. I closed my eyes and felt waves of sheer pleasure washing over me as she burned into my back with permanent ink.

"How did you get into tattooing?"

"Oh, that's a long story," she sighed.

"I'm not going anywhere."

"Guess not, eh? Alright, well, when I was growing up, we lived right downtown, by Much Music."

I nodded, pretending I knew where that was. I had never been to Ontario, but I knew an awful lotta JAFFOs.

"Mom worked twelve-hour shifts at Toronto General," Sonya said, wiping away ink.

"Your mom's a doctor?"

"Nurse."

"Oh."

"So she was either sleeping or working. I could do pretty much whatever I wanted. I met a bunch of people who were into a lot of crazy scenes. Punk, goth, kink, tattoo."

"Hot."

"I was hanging out with these graffiti artists and learned a lot from them, started doing more and more of my own stuff. Some of my graf art is still around, I think."

I couldn't see her face, but I could tell she was smiling. She grabbed a new wad of paper towel to wipe with. I had a mirror set up so I could see what she was doing on my back. I was bleeding quite a bit, and I felt bad about that.

"I was never squeamish about blood and needles and shit, so I was either gonna be a nurse or a tattoo artist, I guess." She laughed. I realized that I hardly ever heard Sonya laugh and I wished I could make her laugh more often. "What does your mom think about you tattooing?"

"She hates it. She thinks tattoos are for circus freaks and whores."

I nodded.

"Don't move," Sonya said.

"Sorry. Go on."

"She disowned me for a while. After she saw my first tattoo, she right flipped, man. Tried to scrub it off my foot with an SOS pad. When she realized it wasn't coming off, she ran around the house screaming and crying like a banshee, packed up all my shit, told me to get out of her sight, that I disgusted her."

"Harsh."

"She raised me Jewish."

"Oh."

"People with tattoos aren't allowed to be buried in a Jewish cemetery."

"I know."

"So, that was . . . hard."

"I bet." So Sonya was a Jew. I guess I could convert for her. But wait, would that mean I'd have to chop off my foreskin? I closed my eyes, tuned in to the sensation of the needles penetrating my upper back. There was a lotta heat happening back there. It was euphoric, in a way. I never wanted her to stop.

"I went to OCAD while I was living with my mom, but when she kicked me out I couldn't afford to pay rent and tuition, so I dropped out. I was only one year away from graduation."

"That sucks."

"Whatever, most of those artsies are fuckin pretentious assholes anyways. I don't need a piece of paper to tell me I'm an artist."

"I think you're a brilliant artist."

"Thanks. I think you're a prick."

"Thanks."

Neither of us said anything for a while. I listened to the hypnotic buzz of the machine and enjoyed the feeling of her hands on me as she stretched my skin taut.

"So how did you get your mom to forgive you?"

"I got in a car accident."

"Extreme," I laughed.

"I was on my way back to TO from New York." Her voice seemed far away. "I'd been checking out studios to see where I could apprentice. I was hit by a drunk driver near Niagara Falls."

"Holy fuck, Sonya, were you hurt?"

"Chipped my front tooth and cervical spine."

"Damn." I loved that chip on her tooth, it was super sexy.

"Broke three ribs, my collar bone, my left arm and wrist, and I was in a coma for a hundred and eight days."

"Wow, you're lucky to be alive."

"That's what they say." She changed to a bigger shader and the sensation was different, like she was pushing the needles into me deeper now. I bit my lip as she ran the ten mag over my spine. "Luckily, I didn't suffer much brain damage, just some memory loss," she said. "When I came to, I thought I was still on my drive back home, it was like no time at all had passed. I was thinking of stopping for a coffee and some gas. I wanted to get out and look at the falls and stretch my legs."

"Crazy."

"It was weird. I lost that time, you know? Three and a half months of your life. Gone."

"Yeah," I whispered.

"So, it took about a year and a half to recover from that one, but at least I learned to be ambidextrous."

"I noticed that. Bet that comes in pretty handy."

"Funny guy."

"I do what I can." I almost shrugged but stopped myself in time. "So what happened after you woke up from your coma?"

"I stayed with my mom and she helped me a lot and we became close again. When I was strong, I decided to check out some tattoo shops out west. I travelled six months in Calgary, Banff, and Vancouver, looking at, talking about, making, and getting tattoos. I took the ferry over to check out Victoria one day and decided to stay for a while."

"And now here you are."

"Here I am, five years later."

I was glad that Sonya had opened up to me, finally. And that she did that phoenix tatt for me gratis. It turned out amazing. Even better than I'd expected. And I expected nothing less than perfection from the Shadow. It's incredible. She's incredible. Her style is unlike anything I've ever seen. She calls it "a radical feminine aesthetic." I call it fucking sweet.

....

I asked Sonya out for beers a few times but she always had some excuse. Like she had a date or she had to meet up with a friend or she had to feed her cat. I don't know. I guess she wasn't into hanging out with her co-workers outside of work. I'm pretty sure she never went out with Hank either. Sometimes I would ask her how her dates went, not that I really wanted to know, except that I did. Badly. I tried to imagine the kinds of chicks she would go out with, but I couldn't get a handle on her type. I figured she was probly super picky, and she deserved to be. She was very secretive about it all and would never give away any hints about who she was going out with. She'd just get this stupid grin on her face when I asked and say, "Fine," or "Pretty nice," or once, "Lame."
"Anyone I'd know?"
"Nope."
"Gonna see them again?"
"Maybe. Maybe not."
"What are you looking for?"
"Oh, you know, I'm just a carefree single lesbo, lookin for love." And she'd shrug and smile while my heart crumbled inside my chest.

....

I'd been apprenticing with Hank about a year and a half by this time. Still hadn't been paid a single cent. Still washing dishes three or four nights a week at the George and still living in the same shitty room upstairs. I was sick of having no money and no time and no girl. And I didn't know when it would end.

One Tuesday afternoon this young Native chick comes into the shop, she wants a tattoo. What does she want? The name of her gang, The Vipers, above her left eyebrow. Pretty bold move, even for a gangster.

I had to laugh. Hank was watching us. The chick was dead serious. She wouldn't hear of alternative placement. It amazed me that she had such dedication to her gang. I realized that if she was ready to show this level of commitment, she would probly die for them too. The Vipers owned her. I looked into her eyes. They were black and set deep in her face. Her eyes were hard and sad and beautiful. I looked at her eyebrows, her forehead, her face.

"I can't give you that tattoo," I said.

She freaked out at me, and I refused again.

"But I'm eighteen!"

"I don't care."

She called me an asshole, then left in a huff.

"You're through," Hank said.

"Seriously?"

"You know the rules."

"You would've done that to her?"

"Get out of my shop."

"Okay."

"Goodfuckinluck to ya."

"Thanks for everything, Hank." I shook his hand.

"Send us a Christmas card." He clapped me on the back, hard.

"Sonya."

"Smell ya later, Ant," Sonya said, looking up from the butterfly she was tattooing.

I missed her already, but I was glad to be done apprenticing under Hank.

....

The sun was shining hot yellow when I walked out so I picked up an eight-pack of Lucky and went to the bagel shop. Kate closed early and we drank beer and hotboxed the bagel oven. I was glad to be free.

"My apprenticeship is officially over."

"Congratulations." She clinked my can. "Cheers, big ears."

"Thanks." I closed my eyes and leaned back into the warm, moist heat of the oven. My body relaxed. I passed Kate the joint and

she smiled at me. I loved her smile because her dimples looked so cute.
I leaned over and kissed her on the cheek.

"Don't do that again," she said.

"Sorry, I couldn't help it."

"That's not my fault."

"Well, whose fault is it then?"

"Yours!"

"I don't see how it's any more my fault than yours."

"It's yours cause you have no self control."

"It's yours cause you're too pretty and sweet."

"Shut up." She hit me in the shoulder and I could tell she
wasn't really mad. I put my arm around her and she leaned in to me as
we finished off the joint.

....

You get to a point in your life when you can look back, look back at
yourself at a certain stage. And sometimes you remember a particular
time as being sort of okay. Sort of good for a while. And you can say,
Yes, I was happy then. Yes. I think I really was. I had done it. I had
gotten in and been trained properly and gotten out and now it was
over. Now I wasn't exactly sure what to do. It was the right time for me
to leave Capital Tattoo, I knew that. I had learned a lot from Hank and
Sonya, but I was ready to start getting paid for my work.

....

I did fuck all for the rest of the week, did a couple dishwashing shifts
and smoked a shitload of weed. I bought a Hustler magazine and
jacked off a lot. I went to three dog fights. At the Friday night fight,
the last dog left standing was faceless and its throat was torn out. I
wondered if its owner would kill it afterwards. I sort of hoped he would.
I mean, that kinda wound doesn't ever heal. But even though I felt bad
about that dog losing its face and all, I went back again the next night,
and the night after that. I made a thousand bucks that week, betting on
the underdog. But I knew I couldn't keep making my money like that.

ashley little

59

prick

It was starting to get to me. I was having more nightmares. Dogs on the street glared at me like they knew.

I thought about where I could work next and wondered if Hank would give me a good reference, if he would recommend me. I wondered if I'd have to do piercing at my next gig as well as tattoo, and I hoped not. I wondered why Hank never taught me scarification, and if he had ever intended to. And I wondered if I would like doing that, or be any good at it. I decided I would try to find someone to learn it from soon. Find out if I liked it. I figured I probly would.

I thought about calling Grace to tell her I'd finished my apprenticeship, but I didn't get around to buying a phone card. Figured it could wait till next week when I got paid.

I had bagels and blow every morning. Kate and I finished off an eight ball over the weekend. Early Monday morning I woke up to someone knocking on my door.

"Who is it?"

"Carmen."

"Finally."

"What?"

"Nothing."

"Phone's for you. It's urgent." Her arm slid around the door and I got up and took the cordless from her. The door clicked shut.

"Hello?"

"Antony, it's Seth."

"Hi."

"Antony?"

"Yeah?"

"Antony, Grace is gone."

"Gone where?"

"She passed last night." His voice cracked.

"Oh." I felt the air rush out of me. I felt like a bowling ball fell on my head. I couldn't breathe. My lungs hurt. My head hurt. Everything hurt. The floor rushed up to meet me. I fell onto the bed. I squeezed my eyes shut. "What did you do to her?"

"Nothing, Antony. I swear to God I didn't touch her, I didn't. It was her heart."

"What's wrong with her heart?"

"It failed."

....

I hung up the phone and got under the blankets and pulled my knees to my chest. I curled in a ball on my side and rocked back and forth, back and forth. I thought maybe if I could go back to sleep then I could wake up again and this wouldn't be happening. Strange sounds were coming out of me. Sounds I didn't recognize. I was cold and scared and so, so tired.

....

I didn't go to Grace's funeral in Calgary. I regret that. I know I should have gone. I should have said a proper goodbye. But I didn't want to see her dead. I just didn't. I wanted to remember her as alive and eternally optimistic. Not as some cakey, made-up corpse in a box.

After about a week and a half of moping around my room like a miserable slob, doing nothing but sleeping and smoking weed, I decided to get a tattoo for Grace. I went to see Clayton at The Skin You're In because I knew he did good work and I didn't want Sonya or Hank to see me like this, I didn't want them giving me a hard time.

I got the words Rest In Peace Grace over my heart inside a cross with black swirls and red roses at each end. Yeah, it hurt. But the pain was good.

My eyes were watering the whole time Clayton worked, but he didn't say anything about it, and I was thankful for that. When it was finished it was amazing how different I felt. Lighter, calmer, more peaceful. I thought that maybe I would be okay now. Maybe this wasn't the end of the world after all.

....

Grace left me twenty-five grand in her will, after all her assets were sold. Guess how much she left for Seth? Zero dollars. God, I love her for

ashley little

61

that. That was the big *Fuck you* that she could never give him in real life. It was her revenge from the grave.

I fantasized for a few days over what I could do with all that cash. I pretty much knew what I really had to do with it right away though.

....

I decided to start my own tattoo shop, be my own boss. So I opened Red Ant Tattoo. You've probly heard of me. I found a perfect rental space in the Fernwood Square. Just a few metres away from the George & Dragon. The rent was obscene but it was a pretty sweet location and a high-traffic area, right next to a pizza place, which also had great coffee. It took about six weeks to get all my equipment, inks, machines, flash, a sign, a card, a cash register, and a business licence.

I remember feeling stupidly excited, like I was walking around in a daze. I remember when my machines arrived by courier, and I had to sign for them. It hit me that this was actually happening. I was doing this. It was the first time in my life I felt like I was doing something real. Something important. Suddenly I couldn't wait to get out of bed in the morning. I'd go to the shop and clean and paint and set shit up and order stuff and basically TCB.

My first day open I was so busy I had to turn people away, get them to make appointments for later in the week. Word about the new studio in Fernwood had spread faster than genital warts, and hordes of people from the Victoria tattoo scene came to check me out. I painted two walls black and two red. I only had one tattooing chair because I could only tattoo one person at a time. I had a little waiting lounge area set up with three soft black armchairs and a black coffee table. On the coffee table I put a photo album with all the tattoos I'd done and some tattoo magazines and some Heavy Metal magazines. There was an ashtray on the table. Like Hank's, it was in the form of a human skull. Unlike Hank's, it was not real. I found it in a pawn shop in Esquimalt. I had snazzy black business cards made up with a red ant in the centre. On the back it said, Anthony Young, Owner Operator, Red Ant Tattoo. I got a real kick out of that. The shop space itself was pretty small—I think six hundred square feet, six-fifty. But it was enough. There was a bathroom. There was a private back room. It was enough. The flash I put up was tasteful, for flash. I didn't put up any of the shit that makes me cringe though, fuck. They'd still ask for it though, eh. Fuckers come in and ask, "Do you have any Winnie the Pooh? Do you have any Yosemite Sam?" And I'd do it, I'd do it. Because that was my job.

....

My opening day was June 1, which was also Grace's birthday, so I thought it seemed right. I know she didn't really like tattoos, but I like to think she would've been proud of me because I was doing something that I actually wanted to do. Something I was good at. And I was doing it on my own. I thought about calling Seth, but I didn't. I know he hated me even more since Grace's estate was settled. He tried to fight it, tried to get something out of me. I don't know how far his mind had slipped by that point, but he was still a fucking warped bastard. Judge denied him, thank Christ. He's probly living in squalor somewhere in Calgary, drinking Alberta Vodka to ease his pain.

Sometimes I wonder why it was Grace who died and not Seth. I mean, she took care of herself, she didn't smoke, she didn't drink, she walked to the Safeway every day and took multifuckingvitamins. And then there's Seth. Smokes a pack a day, drinks at least a mickey a day, usually more, drives drunk all the time and eats doughnuts and KFC! How does that make sense? How is that fair? It doesn't seem right. You know, it's not right. Seth has never contacted me again. It's highly possible that he forgot about me. Wish I could do the same. I'm sure someone will notify me if he kicks it. Pretty sure I'm his only living relative. And, I guess, he's mine.

....

The first four months were pretty busy, probly because it was summer. Since I didn't have another person working the front, I tried to work mainly by appointment only, and I think this added some class to my shop, a certain amount of prestige. So I'd stagger my appointments throughout the day and keep the door open when I wasn't with someone, and usually someone would walk in. Then I'd flip the sign and work on them. It was a pretty good system. I finally quit dishwashing at the George and started sleeping in the needles, as they say. It was alright cause I got a shower installed in the bathroom. And I had two big sinks out front. Got a kettle, a hotplate, a toaster, a bar fridge, and a futon for the back room. Things were cozy. Technically, I wasn't really allowed to be living in there, but it made perfect sense at the time. Made the enormous rent seem more justifiable too.

....

Some things are hard to remember. But, sometimes, tattoos remind me of things I would have otherwise forgotten. Like whenever I see a fish tattoo, I remember this one really hot day when I'd only been open a couple weeks. This middle-aged guy came in whacking around one of those white canes, wearing shades. What the fuck is this? I thought. A blind guy wants a tattoo? What the hell for? I kinda wished there was someone else working with me right then so I could give them the whatthefuckisthis? eyes, but it was just me and I didn't know what to make of this blind guy in my shop. I kinda tested him a bit, didn't make any noise, didn't talk to him for a few minutes. I wanted to see if he was totally blind or if he could tell where I was standing or what. He knew though, he looked right at me when he spoke. It threw me a bit. Well, this guy wanted a big rainbow trout on his forearm. A fantastical one though, with an actual rainbow inside it. I didn't want to offend him, but I had to ask, "Why do you want a tattoo you'll never be able to see?"

"It's not for me." His voice was kinda scratchy and tired.

"Oh, okay, you want a gift certificate then?"

"No, I'm getting the tattoo. But other people can appreciate the colours."

"Okay . . ."

"People love colours. I know they do. The colours make them happy. When they see my rainbow trout, they will smile. So my tattoo is for other people. And even though I can't see it, I'll know it's there. I'll know it's having an effect."

That trout was one of the best tattoos I've done. The colours turned out super bright cause this dude had good fair skin. I liked the literal image too. I ended up making him a raised copy of the stencil, so he could touch it and feel what his tattoo looked like. I took a photo of it for my portfolio, and he's got this huge grin on his face. Priceless.

....

There was a rainbow trout mounted on the wall in the basement of our house. Seth caught it at Sylvan Lake before I was born, and then stuffed it. He was big into taxidermy for a while, before Grace made him give it up. There was a whole animal room in our basement. There was a six point buck, a coyote, a raccoon, a rabbit, a squirrel, a Canada goose, a crow, and the trout. I was mesmerized by their shiny glass eyes, their stiff, hard bodies suspended in their last breath, frozen forever in that moment in time. I would go down there sometimes and just stare at the animals. Get right up close and stare into their dark eyes, eyes that looked so real, too real. Sometimes I talked to them. And sometimes I imagined that they talked back to me. The animals never got me in trouble and they never were mean. Mostly, they just listened.

No one ever went down there except for me. Grace was totally creeped out by them. She said it was unnatural to preserve God's creatures like that. She said it was against His will. Once, when she was angry at Seth for pawning some of her jewellery, she threatened to take all the animals to the dump, and Seth said if she did, then she'd better stay right in there with them. I prayed to the baby Jesus that she wouldn't, and that the animals would stay exactly as they were. I wasn't so sure about God, but I liked to think that the animals were watching over me, keeping me safe.

....

Around the end of September, business started to slow right down. Sometimes one of the old salts would come in to get work. But, man, their skin was so worn and weathered and old, all I could do was drag the needles back and forth across their arms. It was like marking up leather. They always wanted an anchor. Or a pin-up girl.

My favourite skin to tattoo is young blonde women. The ink flows in smooth and the skin stretches easily. Colours appear vibrant and true.

One day in early October this honey blonde breezed through the door, and I was had. Her name was Hannah. Hannah had great skin.

....

For her first tattoo, Hannah wanted her name written down the length of her spine, connected to the mirror image of her name on the other side of her spine. Pretty gutsy for a first tattoo. I knew it would hurt like a bitch, I had to go right overtop of the vertebrae in some places. But she took it, she took it lying down. I noticed a few tears drip onto the floor but, for the most part, she seemed okay.

"You alright, Hannah? You wanna keep going?"

"Yeah. I'm fine. I'm fine. Don't stop."

"We can stop anytime you want. You just say the word."

She took almost four hours of that. Saw it right through to the end. I was sure I'd have to do two sessions with her. I figure that was probly the most painful tattoo I'd done so far. But you'd never know it by her reaction. It sounds weird, but she looked different when she left than when she came in. Somehow older, more sure of herself, serene.

Hannah told me later that she'd wanted that tattoo since she was eight years old. Same backwards and forwards, that was Hannah. She came in about a month later to get another word, imagine, encircling her wrist. I guess she was a Beatles fan or something. Her wrist was delicate and soft. I almost hated to mark it up with a tattoo. But I knew it would look sweet when it was finished. While I was working on the m, I had a vision of holding her down by those pale wrists and hovering above her on my futon in the back room. I think she must've had the same idea, cause that's where we ended up.

Hannah tasted like sugar. The rest of her body was just as

tight and creamy as the skin of her wrist. She asked to stay the night and I said okay.

She traced her nails over the phoenix on my back, sending little tingly zaps of warmth all over my body. "If you could have any super power, what would you want to have?"

I rolled over and looked into her eyes which were green and spackled with gold, layered like kaleidoscopes. "I'd want to be able to see into the future," I said.

"Really? I think that would be boring, you'd never have any surprises."

"Yeah, but I'd always be prepared for what was coming next."

....

Hannah came over a lot, mostly in the afternoons. Sometimes at lunch. She'd bring me coffee. Sometimes we'd get pizza. She'd sit and read Tattoo Magazine while I soldered needles or ordered ink or counted cash. I guess she was my girlfriend. But it was never official.

We had fantastic sex. She basically let me do whatever I wanted to her, and she was down for experimentation. We used condoms for the first couple weeks but then we ran out and didn't bother to get any more.

Hannah didn't talk about herself very much, which was a nice change from other chicks I'd been with who were always blabbing on about themselves. You know, all broadcast and no reception. Hannah liked to ask all sorts of shit about me though. About my life, my past, my plans for the future.

"What's your middle name?"

"Danger."

"Where do your parents live?"

"Nowhere."

"What do they do for work?"

"Nothing."

"What do you mean?"

"They're dead."

"Oh, Ant, I'm so sorry."

ashley little

67

prick

"Why? It's not your fault."
"When did they die?"
"When I was three."
"Do you remember them?"
"Not really."
"That's so sad."
"It's okay."
"Do you miss them?"
"No."
". . ."
". . ."
"What's your favourite colour?"
"Black."
"Black's not a colour."
"What is it then?"
"It's a shade."
"Well, black's my favourite shade then."
"What's your favourite food?"
"Pizza."
"What's your favourite movie?"
"A Clockwork Orange."
"If you could be any animal, what would you want to be?"
"A cheetah."
"Why?"
"Cause they live fast and die young."
"When you were a kid, what did you want to be when you grew up?"
"A cop."
"No way!"
"Gotcha."
"Who's your favourite Spice Girl?"
"What?"
"You know, Spice Girls, the band?"
"Yeah, I know, but what's that have to do with anything?"
"It reveals your psychological make-up."
I laughed. "I don't know, they're all pretty hot."

"Yeah, but if you had to pick your favourite."

"The blonde then, I guess."

"Baby?"

"Yeah?"

"She's my favourite too."

"I guess that means we're soulmates then, eh?"

"Are you making fun of me?"

"Yes."

It mostly went like that and we'd laugh at each other and tickle each other and there was a sort of innocent sweetness about it all. Hannah was my number one fan, for a while.

She liked to party too and one night we got pretty drunk and stoned. It was around one in the morning and I was sitting on a chair rolling up a coco-puff, and she came over and sat in my lap. I put the joint down. She kissed me. She was an excellent kisser. We started fooling around a bit. Then suddenly she pulled away and said, "I want you to tattoo me."

"Right now?"

"Yes! Right now!"

Ah, what the hell? I thought. Could be fun. She wanted two fish swimming in opposite directions on her thigh. The Pisces sign. I let her draw them out while we smoked the joint and then I made the stencil from her drawing. I was too fucked to be doing it right then, but I did it anyways. I made a couple mistakes on the eye of the first fish, and the tail of the second one. I went too deep too, so it bled a lot and it was raised afterwards. I felt shitty about that. I should've said, "No, let's wait till tomorrow." But it was her idea, it was her body. It wasn't the last time I tattooed someone while I was drunk and high either.

....

It was a few days before my twenty-first birthday and Hannah came into the shop with her eyes all pink and puffy. I guess I'd forgotten to lock the door. I was doing a skull with a spiderweb in it on the neck of some junky, and I was paranoid about splattering his blood around. I didn't like doing necks and I didn't like doing junkies, so I wasn't having a very good time.

"I need to talk to you," she said.

"I'm kinda in the middle of something, H." I really didn't want to deal with her crying and snivelling right then. I didn't know how to handle that.

"I'll wait then." She sat in a chair and crossed her arms over her chest.

I wished I could close up and go out somewheres and pretend I wasn't home, or at the shop, or whatever. But I was there, and so was she, and I was almost finished with the spider guy. I knew once I taped his bandage on, I'd have to deal with whatever it was that had made her cry, so I took extra time wrapping up his tattoo and giving him his aftercare instructions. But eventually he closed the door, and I sighed and locked it behind him. I turned to her and said, "What's your problem?"

"I'm pregnant, Ant."

"Oh, fuck."

"Thanks."

"Is it mine?"

She stood up and slapped me. Not too hard, just enough to sting. I thought it was a valid question. Then she fell back in the chair and covered her face with her hands and started to sob. I sat down across from her and stared at her. She looked small and weak and pathetic. There was snot dripping from her nose. I lit a cigarette. "You're gonna be okay. You're not gonna have a baby."

"I'm not?"

"Absolutely not."

"How come?"

"We've been partying, Hannah."

"So?"

"So the baby's probly already fucked up."

"No—"

"It wouldn't be fair to bring it into the world when neither of us are really ready for it."

"But, we could get ready for it."

"I don't think so."

....

There were more conversations after that one, but they all went pretty much the same way. There were late night phone calls and fights and lots and lots and lotsa crying. We had sex only once more and it was different. It was tender. Over the next two weeks I convinced Hannah to have an abortion. And she did.

....

She came in a few days after she had it done to get a butterfly tattoo on her hip. I could tell she'd been crying. She let me choose the colours. I gave her iridescent blue and indigo and black and white. I also gave her a little bit of Tokyo Pink. It was a new ink that I hadn't used on anyone yet. Part of me was unsure about using it because there were no long term studies on it. It glows under black light. A little surprise for Hannah to discover sometime in the future. I knew she would love it.

"I really need this tattoo right now. A butterfly is a symbol of regeneration, new beginnings, transformation, change. You know?"

"Yeah, but it's also just a bug that gets crushed on your windshield."

"You're a real prick, you know that?"

I didn't say anything. The buzz of the tattoo machine filled up the silence between us.

....

It was clearly the only choice, even if Hannah didn't think so. Sometimes I think about it now and wonder what it would have been like to have a child, bring him into the shop, show him how to tattoo. Teach him to skateboard. Bring him to all ages shows. You know, show the little guy what's up. And I can almost picture him in my mind, with Hannah's golden curls and a little laughing, devilish face. But I try not to do that. I know I shouldn't do that. Cause there's no going back now. No re-dos. What's done is done is done. It is what it is. And I know that. And I know I can never go back.

Hannah was a mess after the whole thing and she really let herself go. Stopped showering and all that. She hadn't told anyone she was pregnant and I'm pretty sure no one but me knew she'd had the abortion. She said she regretted her decision every single second of every single day and she never should've let me talk her into it.

"A part of me will always resent you for that," she said, her eyes burning into me, green and cold. There was none of the softness and light that was there before.

"You'll get over it, eventually," I muttered.

"This is not something that you get over, Ant. Abortion is forever."

She said she felt like she just killed someone, someone that she loved. Like she just left him behind on the road to die and kept driving and didn't stop and didn't look back, just kept on driving.

I told her I didn't want to see her anymore. She freaked. She thought we had some sort of connection, that we were in love. But we didn't, we weren't. I've been with heaps of girls just like her and none of them were very special. Hannah turned out to be one of the biggest mistakes of my life.

....

What I didn't know about Hannah was that she was only fifteen. I should've figured it out because she only came to see me around 3:30, or at lunch. That's because she went to fucking Vic High, right across the street from my shop. But I never would've guessed she was that young. Not in a million years. She was way too smart for her age. She was fifteen going on thirty.

Hannah was really angry after everything that happened and I guess she wanted revenge against me, wanted me to suffer. So she reported me to the pigs, because I tattooed her, a minor, without parental consent. She also pressed charges against me for statutory rape. I have to admit, I laughed when I found out, because she was the one who had initiated our first time.

I got a huge motherfucking fine and was forced to close my shop for three months, which, as you can imagine, was really, really bad for business. Rumours were flying around town that I was a rapist and that wasn't so good for me either. I had no idea how I was going to pay off the fine, hire a lawyer, and keep paying rent on the shop while not being able to tattoo.

I lay in bed thinking about Hannah, how she had fucked me over. How I should sue her for slander. Sue her and her family for everything they had. But I knew it wouldn't make anything better. It wouldn't really change anything. Our baby would still be in a bio-hazardous waste container, and my reputation would still be ruined. Fuck it, she wasn't worth the time or the hassle. She was just young, she was just a fucking kid.

....

In the morning I had a wake and bake, then went downtown and bought sheets of thick black poster paper and some clear packing tape. When I got back to the shop I smoked another joint and made some toast. Then I taped the black paper over all the windows and the door. I didn't want anyone seeing me in there since I wasn't legally allowed to be living there. I was going to keep living there though, obviously. I had nowheres else to go. And, besides, it was mine.

With the shop closed, I was bored and depressed and hungry. I wanted the weekend to hurry up and get here so I could go win some dough at the dog fights. I smoked a lotta weed and drew up some new tattoo designs in my sketchbook. I went to the George & Dragon and watched TV on their big screen. If no one was watching the game, I'd get Carmen to switch it to the National Geographic channel. I like watching nature documentaries. I don't know why, but they soothe me. I could watch them for hours. *It's an intoxicating moment, that instant of the lion's explosive and determined rush at its prey. But the water buffalo has an advantage...* Everything always makes sense in nature documentaries. Everything has a purpose. But I couldn't just sit there and watch them all day without ordering anything, so I usually had a few beers. Sometimes Carmen would bring me a little plate of fries if she could swing it. I was dying to ask her out, but she was dating Andrew, the manager, and he was not someone I wanted to fuck with.

So I skated around town and scoped out girls and cars and bikes and boards. I visited Kate at the bagel shop. I hadn't seen her in awhile. Not because I hadn't wanted to see her—I had. But I'd been super busy with the shop and Hannah and all that bullshit. I had missed Kate, and I gave her a hug. She smiled, but she looked tired and sad. She had some green remnants of a bruise around her eye.

"What happened to your eye?"

"Aw, you know, partying too hard, fell into a door knob."

"Bullshit," I said.

"What the fuck do you know?"

"Whoa, sorry I asked."

"I'm sorry. I'm sorry, Ant. I just really need to get high right now. Let's go get high. Please?" She took my arm and tugged me towards the back kitchen.

We did a couple lines together and, for a few minutes, I felt okay again.

"Whew! That's better." She leaned her forehead against my shoulder and I inhaled the cinnamony smell of her hair.

"Are you okay?"

"Yeah," she sighed. "I think so."

"Is there anything I can do?"

She shook her head.

"I could have him taken care of."

She snickered into my chest. "Right."

I put my arms around her and smoothed her hair down with my palm.

"You know, I would never hurt you, Kate."

"I know."

....

Finally, the weekend arrived and I went to the dog fights. But I fucking well wished I hadn't. For one, because I lost everything. Not just one night, but both nights, putting me even deeper in the hole. On Friday night, I lost every fight I bet on. Lost four bills. So I felt like I had to go back on Saturday to win it back, even though I really didn't want to go. I really didn't want to see another dog fight as long as I lived. I was beginning to hate myself for ever being involved in the sport. Plus, the smell in there nearly made me puke. But I had to go, I had to go and try to win it back.

Well, as it turned out, Saturday night was one of the longest, most vicious fights in the history of dog fighting. It lasted nearly five hours. Alls I wanted to do was make my money back and get the fuck out of that hellhole. But I had to watch. I had to watch for four and a half fuckin hours while these immaculate animals ripped each other apart. A few guys left before it was over, forfeited their bets. I wanted to leave too, I really did. But I couldn't afford to. Finally, *finally*, around 4:30 in the morning, it was over. One dog was disembowelled and the other one was dead. And I couldn't help thinking that it was all just such a waste, you know? Such a goddamned waste.

The next night, I briefly thought about going back to try to recover some of what I'd lost. Over six hundred dollars. And I was not in a position to be losing money. But I couldn't bring myself to do it again. I felt sick when I thought of going. And, you know, as much as I wanted and needed that money back, it wouldn't have been worth it. Even if I'd won a million bucks, it wouldn't have been worth it.

....

Instead, I waited around for another idea to present itself. I wanked around till Wednesday, then went down to Capital Tattoo to see Hank. I figured he'd know what to do. I brought him an extra large coffee, lotsa cream, lotsa sugar. Sonya was there too, so I gave her my coffee and pretended that I'd already had one. Sonya had some new ink. She pulled her hair back to show me the tiny red rose with a thorny green stem behind her left ear. It was delicate and beautiful and perfect. I asked her who did it. I could tell it wasn't Hank's work. She'd had it done by a chick at the Seattle Tattoo Expo. Some dyke, no doubt. She and Hank were closing up for the day and it looked like they'd been busy.

"Something you need, Ant?" Hank asked, sitting down to roll his 4:20 joint.

"Yeah, actually, I've got a little problem."

"Uh oh," Sonya said, and went into the back room to put the day's needles into the autoclave. When she came back out, the three of us smoked the joint and I told them about the Hannah situation. Hank nodded his head at some parts and grinned like a fiend when it came out that she was only fifteen. "You dirty dog," he said. "Well, you know what I always say, if there's grass on the field, play ball!" He laughed and it sounded like a paper bag ripping open.

When I was finished, Sonya shook her head sadly and said, "That sucks, man." She was wearing black eyeliner that made her blue eyes pop. She was so beautiful it was hard to look at her. I wanted her to hold me and tell me everything was going to be okay. But she crushed her coffee cup in her hand and said she had to go, she was late for a very important date. "Take care of yourself, Ant." She brushed her hand over my shoulder on her way out the door.

"We'll get you through this, kid, not to worry," Hank said, passing me the joint. I took a long hit and let the THC tingles spread through me. I relaxed back into the chair.

"Ever sold drugs before, Ant?"

"Yeah."

"How'd that work out for ya?"

"Shitty. I got caught and had to go to juvie."

"You know how not to get caught now?"

"Yeah."

"Good, cause we got a few pounds of brown to unload right now, and that's not all. Money's not bad if you can manage yourself. Want in?"

This was the split decision that could've gone either way. And everything would have been completely different now if I'd said no.

....

Hank dropped off the stuff the next night at my shop: three grams of heroin, an ounce of coke, and a QP of weed. These guys don't fuck around. Most of it had already been divvied up into small street amounts in tiny plastic bags. Some had skulls and crossbones on them, that was the heroin. Some had eight balls, that was the coke. The weed was in plain Ziplocs. Lucifer's Choice had made it pretty fuckin simple for me. Hank loaned me a scale and gave me the cellphone and the spiel: "No stepping on anything, that's been taken care of, no discounts, no fronting, no credit, and absolutely no getting high on your own supply." Then he took out a little mirror and a little razor and dumped a little heroin onto the mirror and chopped up two teensy tiny little lines for us to sample. "Gotta know your product." Hank winked and snorted up his line. Then he passed me the mirror. The taste in the back of my throat was bittersweet.

"What do you think?"

"This is gonna go quick and easy." I licked my lips.

"Call me to collect the cash once you clear a couple grand," Hank said.

"Okay."

"Your cut is twenty percent."

I nodded.

"Don't fuck up." And then he was gone.

I looked around at all the dope lying on my floor, and I laughed a tight little heroin laugh. Then I collapsed on my futon and stared at the ceiling. I thought my ceiling was very, very beautiful at that moment and so were the walls. They were perfectly bare and this calmed me. Clear space, clear mind. I felt like my futon was a raft and I was floating on a sea of drugs. I smiled, knowing that sea would transform into a boat load of cash for me.

I could re-open in two and a half months. Everything would go back to normal. I could tattoo again, and my name would be cleared. Everything would be okay. Everything would be just fine. Right now, I was just killing time. I felt my body heavy and sinking, dissolving into the futon. I closed my eyes, and was gone.

....

In the morning I woke up with a headache. I went next door to get a coffee, and on my way back inside my shop I saw that someone had scrawled in red spray paint across the door, a word:

RAPIST!

I got this weird liquid feeling in my gut and suddenly felt very ill. My knees turned wobbly and I wanted to sit down right there on the sidewalk. I swore and looked around to see who else had seen it. If I ever find the little fucker who did that, man, fuck. Let's just hope for both our sakes, I never do.

I went inside and got some cash and ran down to the hardware store and got a can of red spray paint. I didn't stop in to see Kate, even though I passed right by the bagel shop, because I didn't want too many people seeing that fuckin monstrosity. It was a Friday, a lotta people would be out. When I got back, there were some people from the neighbourhood standing around looking at the word and pointing and talking. I felt sick. "It's not true!" I announced. "It's not true." They all gave me these harsh stares and I just wanted to curb stomp every one of them for thinking what they were thinking about me. And I wanted to rip out their tongues so they wouldn't tell everyone else in the world what they saw.

I sort of shooed them away and then set to work. I spray-painted the entire door red. The wind blew some of the paint in my eyes, I guess, because my eyes were watering like a fuckin fire hydrant. I couldn't believe someone would do that to me. I know it sounds gay, but I felt so . . . violated. And the worst part of it was, that it wasn't even true. Hannah might not have been an adult, legally, but she was definitely consenting.

I sprayed and sprayed. Flecks of red paint got all over my hands and arms and it looked like I'd been spattered with blood. When I finished, I stood back on the road and looked at the door, the sign, the shop, *my* shop. And, you know something? That red door looked pretty fuckin good. It looked even better than before. It would probly even bring me more business. Maybe the little fucktard who did it had actually done me a favour.

I went inside and made some toast and turned the LC cellphone on. Right away it started ringing, before I could even finish my breakfast. People wanting this and that and that and that and that and this. I wrote down all the places and times we arranged to meet on my hand and then hopped on my skateboard to go deliver. After I closed a deal, I rubbed it off my hand. I didn't have to go too far, most people wanted to meet me downtown. Sometimes they wanted me to come to their house, which I felt kinda weird about, but did it anyways.

The phone rang steadily all day and all the next day too. Some of the customers were sick and dirty with ruined faces and jagged limbs, but some were yuppies, business execs, media moguls, politicians, and parents. People you would never expect to get high, preparing to get really fuckin high.

By Sunday night I had three grand stashed inside a pencil case. I called Hank. He came over about an hour later, and he seemed like he was in a good mood.

"How's it going Hank?"

"Good as, mate," he said. I guess he'd picked that up in New Zealand or something. He sometimes slipped into a Kiwi accent when he'd been drinking.

"Gettin any?"

"Sure am."

"Oh yeah?"

"That's right."

"Who's the latest victim?"

"Gave this sweet little lady a white dragon last night, my boy."

I laughed. Hank's expression changed, and his face flushed. I don't think he liked being laughed at.

"Bet you don't even know what that is," he said.

"I do, I do."

"What is it then, smart-pants?"

"It's when a chick's sucking you off and you cum so hard in her mouth that it comes out her nose. Hence, a white dragon."

"Beautiful thing, isn't it?" Hank leaned back in his chair and lit a cigarette.

We had a little laugh together.

Hank had an old lady named Mandy. She was a washed-up bleach blonde waitress at a cheesy Mexican restaurant. They didn't live together or anything but they'd been dating for seven years or something crazy like that. Sometimes he'd go weeks without seeing her though, and I guess that worked for both of them. I remember she came into Capital for a couple tattoos. Sometimes she'd bring Hank a soft taco or something.

"How's Mandy?"

"Fine, fine."

"She have kids?"

"Yeah, a girl, your age."

"Hm."

"Married."

"Ah." I nodded, thinking how bizarre it was that someone my age could be married.

"So what have ya got for me, Ant?"

I handed him the pencil case and he took the cash out and counted it. Then he put it all into his black bag and stood up to leave.

"Hank?"

"What?"

"Do you think I could get my cut now? I gotta see a lawyer about getting these charges dropped."

"Of course, kid, of course. I thought you already took your cut."

"No."

"Here." He handed me $600. "I'll swing by tomorrow to drop off more product."

"Sure. Hey, Hank, is it always this busy?"

He looked at the wad of cash, then back at me. "For a weekend, that was slow."

....

If anyone ever tells you dealing drugs is easy money, they're a fuckin liar. Dealing is more fuckin hassle than it's worth if you ask me.

In school, when I started getting high, I learned and accepted

the three rules of doing drugs. That sooner or later you're gonna get:
1. Ripped off
2. Caught
3. Sick

When you're dealing, there are different rules. Harder rules. If you're going hard enough and long enough, you will eventually get:
1. Robbed
2. Busted
3. Killed

But the money was good and the drugs were good, so I tried to do my best and keep a low pro, believing that these rules did not apply to me. Dealing was only a temporary arrangement. I knew I didn't want to make a career out of it. There was a lot to learn, and some things I wish I'd never had to.

....

I was hooking Kate up with coke and weed. We were partying together a lot and finally started sleeping together, even though she had a boyfriend. Kate was a tiger, especially when she was high, and I had her all over that bagel shop. It was better than I could've imagined. She was loud and aggressive and hotter than the oven, which we did it in, and let's just say it gave a whole new meaning to the term "hot sex."

After a few weeks of this, I stopped charging Kate for her drugs, but I was still making good money off her because she bought through me for her boyfriend and his friends. I guess you could call it customer appreciation.

She told me her boyfriend used to deal, but got rid of everything when the cops started sniffing around their apartment. She was convinced one of his buddies was the narc, but her boyfriend wouldn't believe her.

"Don't mention my name around them then."

"I'd have to be pretty stupid to do that," she said.

"Unless you want us to get caught." I poked her in the ribs.

"I don't."

Kate would tell her boyfriend she was going out for drinks

with the girls or whatever and then we'd get together for a few lines and usually some beer and a good shag. Sometimes if I had to make a delivery across town she'd drive me there.

One night she drove me to Mount Doug for a big run. I dropped off a couple eight balls and half an o-zee and got back in her car.

"Can we do some now?" Kate asked. Passing headlights illuminated her eyes and they were like drops of liquid gold.

"Sure, babe. Here." I tapped a little bit onto her hand between the thumb and first finger and then did the same. We both snorted the bumps and then she reversed out of the driveway. I leaned over and kissed her on the cheek. A smile spread over her face as she took one hand off the steering wheel and let it rest on my knee. I closed my fingers around hers.

Kate's Civic purred through the city and we were feeling good, flying down Hillside about one in the morning. Suddenly there was a thunk and a jolt and a thud-thud underneath us.

"What the fuck was that?" Kate yelled.

I looked behind us. I could barely see the shape of a human body lying in the road, it was wearing all black. "Oh, shit," I breathed. "WHAT THE FUCK WAS THAT!?"

"I don't know."

"What should I do? What do I do?" She was hyperventilating.

"Calm down, keep driving."

"I can't, I can't. We gotta go back. We have to see if he's okay."

"No," I said. I had a shit load of cash and drugs on me, I was facing charges already, I couldn't afford to go back.

"What?"

"We're not going back."

"But—"

"Take a left. We're going to my place."

"Holy fuck, holy fuck, holy fucking Jesus Christ fuck," she chanted under her breath until we pulled up to my shop. She cut the ignition. "What the fuck just happened back there, Ant?"

"Nothing."

ashley little

prick

Kate came inside and I rolled her a fat joint to calm her nerves, but she couldn't calm down and she was pacing all over like a madwoman and tearing at her hair and basically freaking right the fuck out.

"Come here, sit down." I patted the futon beside me. She sat down and I put my arms around her and pulled her in to me and held her tight. I felt her vibrating and then she started to cry. I wanted to tell her that everything would be okay. I wanted to tell her I loved her. But I didn't.

"I didn't see him, I didn't see anybody there," she whimpered.

"I know."

"I didn't mean to."

"I know."

"We should've gone back, we have to go back, Ant!"

"No."

She bit her lip and leaned in to me, I rubbed circles over her back with my palm. The way Grace used to do for me, when I was crying.

"I don't know what to do," she whispered into my chest.

"Don't worry. He's probly just stunned or something."

"Really? You think?"

"Yeah, probly."

We sat like that for a long time and I dozed off for a couple minutes.

"I have to go," Kate said. She stood up.

"You can stay, if you want."

"I can't."

"Kate, I want to wake up next to you."

"I can't."

"Kate?"

She turned back, halfway out the door.

"Don't tell anyone what happened tonight."

She closed the door, and I was alone.

········

I bought the *Times Colonist* every day after that for two weeks and scanned for anything about a hit and run, something on Hillside, a mysterious death, anything. I knew it was wrong what we did, but I never saw anything in the paper about it, and eventually the weight in my chest began to subside. I didn't leave the shop very much during that time, except when I had to make deliveries. I felt like people were staring at me in an accusing way. Sometimes I thought people on the street were whispering about me. Word had gotten out about the stat rape charges and there was a lotta speculation flying around about what had gone down between me and Hannah. And also about why my shop was closed. I heard that some people were saying it was shut down due to unhygienic or unsafe practices, which really pissed me off. I wish I could have shown them my Universal Precautions and Blood Borne Pathogens exam, which I scored 100% on. I was safe. I was clean. But my reputation in Victoria was permanently tainted.

....

About a month later, I saw a poster tacked up on a telephone pole by the Hillside Mall:

DO YOU HAVE ANY INFORMATION ABOUT A HIT AND RUN THE NIGHT OF NOVEMBER 11 ON HILLSIDE RD? CALL 721-1981 OR CRIMESTOPPERS.

I looked around to see if anyone was watching, then ripped the poster down. I really wanted to call the number to find out if the guy was alright, but I didn't. I didn't call, I didn't tell Kate about the poster, and I never saw another one. I never heard anything about it again and, for the most part, I've put the whole thing out of my mind.

....

I was drinking a lot and doing a lotta drugs. Sometimes with Kate, sometimes with Hank, sometimes with the people I dealt to, sometimes alone. I was making decent cash and had hired a lawyer to bail me out of the Hannah situation. He charged me $590 to make a few phone calls, but eventually Hannah decided to drop the statutory rape charge against me, which was possibly the biggest relief of my life. Made me wonder how many innocent guys get barred for shit they didn't even do, you know? Like, how many blameless guys are sitting in their cells right now, waiting for their parole, thinking: *Man, did I really do that? No, I sure as fuck didn't. But I might as well have, because everyone else thinks I did, and I'm sure as shit gonna get punished for it anyways.*

It's fucked up. They call it justice. I call it convenience.

It wasn't like Hannah was a virgin when I met her. I'm pretty sure she wasn't, anyways. I didn't force her into anything, that's for damn sure. I was so angry that she'd damaged my reputation. I hated that I would always be known to strangers as "the tattooist who raped that girl," even though it wasn't true. It wasn't true at all.

....

I usually go to the laundromat on Sundays. There was this gothic chick I ran into all the time there. We never really talked much, but we had sort of a nice thing going on. We would always give each other the nod. We'd smoke cigarettes outside under the awning while we waited for our laundry to dry. I'd draw in my sketchbook, she'd write in her journal. It was nice, you know? It was comfortable. She usually had candy with her, and she'd offer me some. She commented on my tattoos a couple times. When I was in the process of doing my sleeve, she said it looked like it was coming along nicely or something encouraging like that. She had three black circles tattooed on both her wrists. I never asked her what they were about. I figured she was into witchcraft or some shit.

Then, after all the bullshit with Hannah got out, I walked into the laundromat one day and she was sitting on a washer, eating Gobstoppers. As soon as she saw me, she bolted. Grabbed her purse and out the door. No nod. No candy. No smoke. No eye contact. Just gone. Fast as she could get out of there. Fucking *gone*. I mean, I didn't really know her, we weren't friends or anything, but, Christ, what *was* that?

Her clothes were in the dryer. I knew they were her clothes, cause they were all black. And all I could do was just plop down and watch them. I sat on a plastic chair and watched her clothes spin around and around like a black vortex. I felt a sharp pain deep inside my chest that I could not release.

Goth chick didn't come back for her clothes while I was there. She must have waited me out. Haven't seen her since. I know it sounds kinda weird but, I miss her. I miss doing my laundry with her. I wish I could have told her, *It's not true. Don't believe them. I would never do that. I'm not a rapist. I'm a good person.* But I never got the chance. And now, it's too late.

When the dryer was finished with my clothes that day, I went home and sniffed a line of heroin. Then I made my bed and put my clothes away and lay down on my bed and finally my chest stopped hurting and my head stopped hurting and my sheets were so soft and smelled so good that I just didn't care anymore.

....

The funny thing about junkies is just because you get high with them a couple times, they think you're their buddy, they think you can waive the fee for their last couple of bags. Like dope just grows on trees or something. I had this one customer, Jesse, who was a nice enough guy, fuckin funny too, but he never had any money. He worked for Telus and had a $200-a-day habit. For some reason, I couldn't say no to him. Something in his voice, it was just so desperate. And his eyes were warm and pleading like a puppy's. So I kept bringing him the good Afghani brown and he'd say, "I can pay you tomorrow, I can pay you next week, I can pay you when my cheque comes on Friday."

Finally, I stopped bringing him dope, but the guy still owed me around five grand. He called almost every day, but I told him I couldn't bring him anything until he paid in full. I couldn't afford to front the money to Lucifer's Choice for him, and I was gonna be fucked up the goat-ass unless he coughed it up right quick. I got together with Hank for a few beers one night and asked him what I should do.

"For fuck's sake, Ant, what'd I tell you? Nobody gets credit."

"I know, I know, I thought he was good for it though."

"Junkies are good for nothing."

"He's a decent guy, Hank."

"You know where he lives?"

"Yeah."

"Good. You're gonna unfuck this."

....

So, the next day, that's what we did. Jesse was at work. His dog was in the backyard, a big brindle mastiff that was gentle as hell and nudged us both for a pat on the head. Hank threw his weight against the back door and we walked into the house. It smelled like dog food and cigarette butts. There was really nothing of value in there that we could take to pay off Jesse's debt. He had three big bookshelves crammed with books, but no electronics. He'd probly pawned all his shit long ago. I pulled a book off the top shelf and read the title: *How to Win Friends and Influence People*. I put it in my backpack, I don't know why. I put it in.

"This poor bastard's got fuck all," Hank said.

"I noticed."

"Guess you gotta leave him a warning then." He nodded his head in the dog's direction.

"I do?"

"Come on, Ant, you can't keep letting this douchebag get away with this shit. Nobody fucks with us. He's gotta pay up. Or else you'll have to pay for him."

"But—"

"Are you gonna pay for him?"

"No."

"Then you know what you need to do." Hank took a silenced .32 out of his waistband and handed it to me. I held it and looked at it.

Felt the smooth, cold metal in my hand, the weight of it, surprisingly light. Hank held the door open and whistled once and the dog ran inside. He came running right up to me, all curious and friendly. His coat was shiny orange and brown, tiger striped. He was wagging his tail and looking up at me expectantly. I realized Jesse probly took better care of his dog than himself. I stood there with the gun in my hand and stared at the dog. I looked at Hank. He nodded. I looked at the dog. I didn't think I was capable of this. I liked Jesse. I liked his dog. But I needed the money, and I knew I would get hurt if I didn't get it. I had to do it. I had to, or I would've been royally fucked.

I pulled back the safety and pulled the trigger and shot the dog in the head at close range. He fell sideways onto the carpet, doggie brains splattered all over the white wall behind him. I dropped the gun on the table and walked out the door. I felt cold and mean and sick. I stepped in a big pile of dog shit on my way out of the yard.

....

Hank slid into the driver's seat, started the engine, and pulled out a joint as if nothing had happened. We smoked it on the way back to my shop. But it didn't make me feel any better. My hands wouldn't stop shaking.

Hank looked at me and exhaled a big cloud of smoke between us. "You alright?"

"Not really, man. That was too fucked."

"Well, the world's a cesspool, Ant. If you're gonna get in over your head, you better fucking well learn how to swim."

....

When Hank pulled up to my shop, I ran inside and threw up. I got down on my knees and closed my eyes. I saw the dog's eyes, curious, pleading. Then, its bloody, pink brains spewed across the wall. I threw up again. And again and again and again. Until there was nothing left inside me. I rested my forehead against the cold porcelain of the toilet bowl, stained yellow with piss. My body trembled violently while the back of my throat burned acrid and horrible. Snot poured into the toilet. I dry heaved again, nothing. I was covered in a thin layer of cold, slimy sweat. I wiped a pubic hair out of my eye. I stared into the bowl. Little gobs of bile blossomed in the toilet like dandelions.

How did I get here?

I spat out a wad of dark phlegm and flushed. Then I rinsed my mouth and brushed my teeth. I made a cup of tea and drank it, then got into bed. I dug my fingernails into my skin as hard as I could. But I still couldn't cry.

I wanted to blame somebody for what I'd done, what I'd become. In my head, I went through every person I'd ever known. But it wasn't any of them. It was no one else's fault. It was me. It was all me. I rocked back and forth, back and forth, for a long, long time, until finally, I nodded off. I dreamt of the dog's head floating above me, and then it turned into Grace's head and she was crying. I woke up drenched in sweat, my face wet with tears.

....

Jesse paid off his full debt two days later. In cash. He wouldn't meet my eyes. I knew he adored that goddamn dog, and if I could bring it back to life, I would.

Telus workers went on strike a little while after that, and I never heard from Jesse again. I still have dreams about that day. Sometimes the dog explodes when I shoot it. Sometimes I shoot Hank instead. Sometimes I am the dog.

....

I had to call Hank to come over and collect the cash. I didn't feel like seeing him, but I wanted Jesse's money out of my sight. As soon as Hank stepped in the door I could tell he had something eating him. I gave him the money and he nodded and put it away.

"I got an important job for you, Ant."

"Yeah?"

"Four grand in it for you."

"What do I have to do?"

"Make a delivery."

"Okay . . ."

"To Edmonton."

"Oh." I hate Edmonton.

"Here's the deal: you're gonna take a hockey bag on the Greyhound. You're gonna get off at the bus depot in Edmonton and put the bag in a locker there. Locker number one-two-three. There's a combination lock on it. The combo is six-six-six. Then you're gonna get back on the bus and come straight back to Vic. Do not pass go. Do not collect any fucking thing. You get half the money when you leave and the other half when you get back."

"When do I have to leave?"

"First bus tomorrow morning."

"What's in the bag?"

"Don't worry about that."

"But don't I—?"

"No. You're on a need to know basis and you don't need to know. You don't want to know. All you have to do is move it from A to B. What's inside is irrelevant."

"Well, am I gonna have to worry about dogs sniffing around or what?"

"Nope."

"Edmonton, Hank? I fuckin hate Edmonton."

"Hey, can you do this or what?"

"I guess so."

"Well, can you or can't you?"

"Yeah, I guess."

"Good."

....

Well, what the hell? I could sit on a bus for fifty hours for four grand. Money always comes in handy. And I could get the fuck outta Dodge for a bit. Get a change of scenery. I picked up the bag from Capital Tattoo at 10 a.m. and took a cab down to the bus station on Douglas.

I heaved the bag into the trunk. It probly weighed around thirty pounds or so. It was black and bulky and actually felt like there were hockey pads in it. There was one of those cheap mini combo locks on it that you could cut open with a butter knife. At the bus station the cabbie reached for the bag before I could and my heart leapt into my throat. But then I thought, *Who cares? For all he knows, it's hockey equipment in there. What's he gonna do? Call the Iranian embassy on me? You gotta relax, Ant. Be cool, motherfucker, be cool.*

I bought my ticket with cash and the dog-faced lady at the wicket said, "Have a nice trip."

"Yeah, right." As if anyone could have a nice trip to Edmonton.

I went to the can and then had a smoke and then lined up for my bus. I hate waiting in lineups and always have. I finally got to the front and the bus driver had eyebrows like black caterpillars. He looked like he had put on a lotta miles.

"That yours?" He nodded at the bag.

"Yeah"

"It's gotta have a tag."

"Oh."

"They're inside."

"Okay."

"Make it quick, eh? I'm already running behind schedule."

I got a tag and borrowed a pen from some old lady and wrote my name on the tag and ran back out and the driver was all loaded up and ready to go. I attached the tag with my name on it to the bag. My real name. I had a weird feeling doing that. Maybe I shouldn't have put my real name. I had no fucking idea what was in there. It could have been anything. But it was too late.

"Where you going?" the bus driver yelled in my face over the noise of the station.

"Edmonton." I gave him my ticket.

"Hop on." He threw the bag in the middle compartment, on top of everyone else's suitcases and backpacks and boxes. I got on the bus.

....

The bus was full of the usual scum of the earth who ride buses: old guys in sports jackets with bottles of whisky in paper bags, young guys with their cellphones and their iPods, welfare mothers with their screaming babies, touring washed-up strippers. Buses are always so depressing. Especially around Christmas time, which this was. I went to the back and sat beside a fat emo chick who looked like she wanted to stick her head through the glass window. I hoped she wouldn't talk to me and she didn't. She didn't even smile at me. And I was glad. Her stomach flesh was spilling over the armrest into my seat, and I hoped she would sit somewhere else after we got off the ferry so I could have the whole back seat to myself. I tried to be really annoying and drum my fingers and tap my feet and hum a little bit, but she was probly too busy thinking of ways to kill herself to notice me.

It didn't take too long to get to the ferry and I was so glad when we boarded because I was starving. I got in another lineup and got a BC burger and fries with gravy and a Caesar salad and a Coke and a chocolate muffin. It was delicious. Then I did a few laps around the ferry to check out the goods on board. Quite a lotta hot chicks ride the ferry, but they're all those high-maintenance, snobby-ass Vancouver chicks with dogs in their purses and $500 haircuts who won't even give you the time of day on their diamond encrusted watches. Or else they're those fuckin hippie island chicks wearing three million skirts and tea cosies on their heads, and you just know they haven't showered for weeks. Never really met anyone worthwhile on a ferry. I've always wanted to get a blow job on a ferry though. It's a little fantasy of mine.

I went to the outside starboard deck and had a smoke and watched the seagulls suspended in the air, keeping time with the ship. I wondered what was inside the bag. I went to the gift shop and bought a couple magazines for the ride and a bag of dill pickle chips and some water and some Coke. I bought a crossword book just for the hell of it. I used to really like doing crosswords when I was a kid, and I hadn't done one for years. Seth liked them too. That's probly the only thing we had in common.

He would sit at the kitchen table, drinking a glass of vodka like it was water, and he'd holler to me wherever I was in the house, "What's an eleven-letter word for flying dinosaur?" or "What's a

cheese with nine letters?" or "What's an eight-letter word for a star?"
And I would stop drawing or eating or playing Super Mario Bros. or
whatever I was doing and count out the letters on my fingers. Afraid
of getting it wrong and screwing up his whole crossword. He did it in
pen. I did it in pencil.

"Celebrity?"

"Oh *that* kind of star." And he would try to pretend like he
knew the answer all along and he was just testing me, but we both knew
I was better at the longer words because his spelling was shit.

Anyways, I bought a crossword book. Then I sat down on
one of those leather massage chairs outside the gift shop and it talked
to me. It told me to put a dollar in it, so I did. Best dollar I ever
spent. It was so good, I spent another one. And then another one. And
then a toonie. I probly put fifteen bucks into that stupid chair. Then
some kids walked by and started giggling and I kinda started awake
and I think they were laughing at me because I got so relaxed that my
mouth was hanging open. But I guess they could have been laughing at
anything, cause that's what kids do.

The horn was so loud, so loud it made my whole head hurt. Even my
teeth. Then the stupid recorded chimes and the stupid announcement:
"We are now approaching Tsawwassen Ferry Terminal!" I went to the
can and then made my way back down to the vehicle deck. There were
five buses all parked together and they all looked the same. What if
I got on the wrong bus and the bag wasn't on it? What if I didn't go
to Edmonton and the bag did? What if I went to Edmonton and the
bag didn't? Fuck. Fuck! FUCK! Relax. There's the hungry caterpillar
driver. There's your bus. I got on and walked to the back and the emo
chick wasn't there so I put my magazines and my food on her seat and
closed my eyes for a minute.

When I opened them again we were crawling through
Vancouver. People on the streets were drinking out of Starbucks cups
or holding out Starbucks cups, begging for change. There were lotsa
cyclists wearing spandex and shiny helmets, looking like they were from

the future. Pathetic Salvation Army Santas stood on the sidewalks and clanged their miserable little bells. There were too many people and too many vehicles. The seat beside me was still empty and I intended to keep it that way. I saw the time bursting in orange and red as we passed a flashing sign for a funeral home. Only eighteen hours to go.

....

The sky was navy as we pulled out of Coquitlam. I wished I'd brought a few joints for the ride. Or a few lines. Or a bottle of Fireball. Something. Anything. Why hadn't I brought anything? I was a fuckin idiot for not bringing anything. What the hell was wrong with me? I wasn't thinking. Alls I could think of was that goddamn hockey bag. What was in it? Who was getting it? Who knew it was coming? I needed something to take the edge off. Every time I heard sirens, I thought they were coming to haul me away for whatever it was I was transporting. Maybe this was a set up. Maybe this was the way Hank got rid of his competition. Maybe he had this planned all along. But no, that's crazy. Hank's your friend. Hank's a good buddy. Isn't he?

....

In Chilliwack I had a heart attack. A cop behind the bus put his siren on and *oh no oh no oh fucking fuck jesusfuckingchristalmighty I. Am. So. Fucked.* I slumped down in my seat. Put my hood over my head. This was it. This was fucking *it.* I was going to prison for life. No bail. No hearing. No chance of parole. And I'd only made it to The Wack. FUCK! I could see the lights flashing blue-red, blue-red. The bus pulled over to the shoulder and I thought I might start to cry. Fuck you, Hank, for getting me to do your dirty work. Why me? Why not one of your Choice boys? This is wildly fucked. This is right fucked up. I should've said "No." I should've said "Do it yourself." I should've said "Go fuck yourself." I should've said "Do I have a big FedEx tattoo on my forehead? NO! I DON'T! BECAUSE I AM NOT A FUCKING COURIER SERVICE!" Now I'm fucked. I am beyond fucked. I am royally fuckin fucked right up the goat-ass. I wanted to go into the bathroom to hide but the red occupied sign was on. I thought I might piss my pants.

The bus door opened and the overhead lights came on and I could feel the cold air shoot right to the back of the bus and up my nostrils. The cop climbed on and my heart stopped. He talked to the driver and showed him something. A poster or a photo or something. The driver shook his head. I strained to hear what they were saying.

"Mind if I have a look around?" the cop asked.

"Sure thing, but try to be quick, eh? I'm running behind schedule."

"Sorry to hold you up, folks," the cop announced. "We're just looking for someone, and then we'll have you on your way."

There was some commotion among the passengers and I noticed another guy ducking low and turning his ball cap around. I looked around at the other passengers and wondered how many people on the bus were thinking the exact same thing I was. The cop walked up the aisle, slowly coming towards me. I grabbed a magazine and buried my face in it. Be cool. Be cool. Be cool. I pretended to read. I squeezed my legs together so I wouldn't piss myself. I looked up and gave him a little nod when he got to me. He paused for a second too long. *Fuck. Me. Here we fucking go.* I held my breath. Then he spun on his heel and started walking down the aisle. I let out my breath. My heart dove into my stomach and then exploded. I had been spared. I looked out the window. The streetlights lit up the snow that had just started to fall. It twinkled and sparkled in the night.

"Thanks, folks, sorry for the delay. Happy holidays." The cop gave us a wave and stepped off the bus.

It took about half an hour for my heart rate to return to normal. I tried to do a crossword, but I couldn't concentrate. I watched the woman in the aisle across from me do her makeup using a compact mirror. She had white-blonde hair, she was probly thirty-fiveish, probly a stripper. There was something soothing about watching her put her makeup on. She was very efficient. She caught me staring at her and gave me a little smile as she clicked her compact shut and tucked it into her purse. I turned away. I pressed my face against the cold glass of the window and watched my breath fog it up. My head hurt. I was thirsty.

I just wanted to get there. Dump the bag. Get out. I wanted this to be over and I never wanted to do anything like this ever again. I closed my eyes for a while but couldn't sleep.

After Kamloops, all the overhead lights went out and the bus was dark and quiet. I needed to get to sleep and I needed to relax. I looked around. No one was awake, except for a Native woman who was nursing her baby. I looked over at the stripper. She had her mouth open and her lips were pink and glistening. I unzipped my pants and took out my cock. I stroked it lightly at first, then faster and harder. I watched her chest rise and fall with her breathing and I imagined my dick in her pretty little mouth. Faster and faster and faster and then I opened the flap of the seat pocket ahead of me and came inside of it. Then I put myself away, leaned back in the chair, closed my eyes, and fell fast asleep.

....

When I woke up, we were stopped in Jasper and the day's first light was illuminating the mountains. I had been to Banff before, but never to Jasper. I thought Jasper was nicer. It didn't make me feel claustrophobic the way Banff did. I walked around for a bit and stretched my legs. My feet and ankles felt swollen, my back was stiff and sore. I got some water and some coffee and a lemon Danish and sat on a bench facing the mountains and smoked a cigarette. The stripper came over and sat down on the bench. I felt a hot blush rising up my neck, but I figured she wouldn't notice.

"Do you have a light? Mine just quit."

I handed her my lighter.

"Thanks." She took a silver cigarette case out of her purse, opened it, and sparked a little joint. I could see her body getting more and more relaxed with every puff. She leaned back into the bench and blew a long thin stream of smoke towards the mountains. "You want some?" She held out the joint to me.

"Thanks." I took a few hits and instantly felt better.

"Where are you headed?"

"Edmonton."

"Me too." She reached for the joint.

"Sorry."

"Yeah," she laughed. "Why are you going there?"

"Business trip."

"Me too. What business are you in?"

"The tattoo business."

"Oh, awesome!"

We didn't say anything for a few minutes. A couple of deer casually crossed the road in front of us. I watched their fragile legs and long necks. I thought about how I liked girls the most when they hadn't said a word yet. As soon as they talked, they screwed up everything. The bus rumbled to a start and the deer skittered away.

"Better get going," she said, squishing out the joint on the bench. She put the roach back in her silver cigarette case.

"Thanks for the hoot."

"No problem."

We got back on the bus.

....

The rest of the ride was a lot easier now that I was high. I could enjoy the scenery as the sun came up. I even saw some more wildlife. Some bighorn sheep climbing up the side of a rock. They were funny looking, and I laughed under my breath. The snow at the sides of the highway was dirty as shit and I was glad that we didn't get snow in Victoria.

I had a lotta time to think on that bus ride, in between panic attacks, and I decided that if I made it back to Victoria in one piece, I was going to tell Kate that I loved her. I didn't care if she said it back. I just wanted her to know. In case something ever happened to me. At least she would know.

I'd never been so happy to see the *Welcome to Edmonton* sign. I had made it. The roads were filthy with slush and the sky was grey and flat and the buildings were grey and looming above us like giant gravestones and the people on the street were grey and ugly and desperate and cold. But I was here. I had made it.

The bus pulled into the depot and I started getting anxious

ashley little

prick

again. What if the cops were waiting inside for me? What if someone else was waiting inside for me? What if I wasn't supposed to ever make it back to Victoria? What if the bag had torn open and the contents were spilled all over the bus? What if it had been damaged? What if it was lost?

The brakes screamed and the driver got out and began unloading baggage. I pushed my way up to the front and got off the bus and grabbed that fuckin hockey bag and ripped the tag with my real name off it and stuffed the tag in the garbage. I went inside the station and it was crowded as fuck, people everywhere, all wanting to go someplace else. I went to the can and dragged the bag into the stall with me so no one would take it or even think about taking it. I stared at the bag. The bag just sat there. It was a little dirtier but otherwise looked the same. I tried the zipper because I wanted to know. The crappy little lock was still secure. I got out my knife. Then someone else came into the bathroom. I froze. He went into the stall beside me. Fuck it. I don't need to know. I put away my knife.

I wandered around the station, lugging the bag over my shoulder like some fucked up Santa sack. Finally, I found the lockers. I found number 123. It was a big bottom one. It was red. What was the combination? Oh fuck. Think. What was it? Shit. I was so tired I couldn't remember. Should've written it down. I got a drink of water from the fountain. It tasted like chlorine. I hate Edmonton. Think. Think. Think. Think. Nothing. Blank. Fuck. Wait, it was something evil. Something about hell. Or the devil. 6-6-6. Mark of the beast. The lock opened and I jammed the bag in. I gave it a few kicks and it was packed in there tight. I slammed the door and locked the lock and changed the numbers on it and walked away. There was no one else around, no one even watching me. I walked away.

....

The next bus for Victoria left in twenty-seven minutes. I bought my ticket then went outside for a smoke and the hairs in my nostrils froze and my lungs seized up. Edmonton was fucking freezing. I fucking hate Edmonton. I couldn't even finish a whole cigarette because I only had a hoodie on. I threw my smoke on the ground and went back inside and got a Teen Burger and a root beer and onion rings from A&W and sat in a booth and ate.

Seth used to take us out to A&W once in awhile if he was in a good mood and had a little extra cash. Grace would get a Mama Burger and he'd get a Papa Burger and I'd get a Teen Burger. Not because that's who we were, but because those were the burgers we each liked the best. I think Grace really enjoyed going out. Probly because she knew she was safe if she was out, that he wouldn't start into her or anything with people around. She would always wear lipstick when we went out anyplace. Even if it was just to A&W to get burgers, she would put on her lipstick. Seth and I would make fun of her for that sometimes, but I don't think she cared.

I finished eating, then went to the can and splashed some water on my face and looked at myself in the mirror. I looked like shit. And I knew I'd look even worse after riding the bus for another twenty-three hours. But, hey, at least I'd be up four grand. I really didn't want to get back on the bus, but I sure as fuck didn't want to stick around Edmonton either. I got back on the bus.

....

I sat at the back again and wouldn't let anyone take the seat beside me. I curled up across the two seats and used my hoodie as a pillow. Twenty-two hours and fifty minutes and I'd be back in Victoria. If we were on schedule. If there wasn't a snowstorm that caused accidents that delayed traffic on the Coquihalla for sixteen hours. Well, I had a lotta time to think anyways. There's something about the rhythm of the road under you and the landscape passing by all around that really makes your mind unravel.

I was feeling fucked. And I was entitled to feel fucked after what I'd been through the last few weeks. Sometimes I had these flashes where I felt like I was watching myself from above. And I wondered how I could be doing the things that I was doing, the things that I'd done. Sometimes, for brief moments, I got this overwhelming fear of what I'd become. It was a heavy feeling, weighing me down. I had this nagging suspicion that I wasn't quite in control of my own life. That I was a puppet, and someone else was pulling the strings. And maybe I didn't like what they made me do, maybe I thought it was wrong, but there wasn't a goddamn thing I could do about it.

But those flashes didn't come very often and I just kept on doing what I was doing without giving too much thought to the consequences. I did know that I'd never do another long distance delivery for Hank, or anyone else, no matter how much they were paying. It wasn't fuckin worth it. Even on the way back when I had nothing on me, I was still paranoid, still looking over my shoulder the entire time.

I fell asleep in Alberta and woke up in BC. When we stopped in Clearwater I got out for a smoke and this sketchy motherfucker came up to me, got right in my face. His teeth were all brown and rotted out, classic meth head, eh. Fuckin disgusting. I don't really take that great of care with my dental hygiene, like I don't floss or anything, I probly don't even deserve to have the teeth that I do, because they're good, straight teeth. I've never even had a cavity. They'll probly be stained yellow with coffee and cigarettes in another twenty years, but they're good for now. Anyways, this meth head came up to me, obviously tweaking, and he asked me if I had his wallet. And he's feeling around in his pockets, his jeans pockets, front and back, his shirt pockets, his jacket pockets, he keeps checking all his pockets, checking checking checking and then checking them all again. It was kinda funny, in a sad sort of way.

"Do you know where my wallet is, brother?"

"No, I don't."

"Well, can you help me look for it? I lost it."

"No, I can't."

He looked at me like I'd just hit him. "What do you mean?"

"I mean I can't help you look for your wallet."

"Why not?" He kept on checking his pockets again and again. His face was covered in pockmarks, greasy brown hair jutted out under his toque. I think meth is gross and stupid and anyone gross and stupid enough to try it more than twice deserves what they get. The bus started up and I flicked my cigarette into a pile of dirty snow.

"Because I gotta get back on the bus."

About twenty minutes later I guess he found it and he held it up for the whole bus to see and screeched, "I found it! I found my wallet!" And I was happy for him, I really was.

....

At some point near Hope I felt like I had been riding the bus for my entire life. That's how long that fuckin bus ride was. It felt like I might never get off. But I knew that soon enough, I would be on the ferry. And I started looking forward to that massage chair again. And a BC burger. And the smell of the ocean. And soon enough, I'd be home, and I could have a shower and roll a fat joint and forget all about the bus. Forget all about Edmonton.

....

When I got back to Vic I went straight over to Broad Street to see Hank and collect the rest of my money. He gave me the cash in a brown envelope and I put it in my pocket. I didn't count it in front of him like I should have, I just put it in my pocket. I wanted to be done with it. Hank asked if I'd had any problems and I said no and he said good. He said a few things had changed since I left, and that he was setting me up with a different supplier, an associate.

"Is he LC?"

"No. He's an *associate*. Like you."

"Oh."

"Okay with that?"

"Yeah, sure, sure. Your call."

"Goddamn right it's my call."

My new supplier was a guy named Michael. He lived in a richie-rich neighbourhood called Golden Oaks.

....

Michael was a chill guy and we ended up hanging out once in awhile but, for the most part, ours was a business acquaintance. I remember one day he'd just gotten some primo honey oil and we got super baked with his roommate, Alex, and together we drove out in Michael's Jeep to play disc golf in the forest. Just for the fun of it. That was a really good day. It was raining a bit, but warm and sunny at the same time, reminded me of that CCR song. Little rainbow patches were shimmering through the trees.

My aim was pretty bad, probly because of the oil's effects, but they didn't tell me I sucked shit or anything. When my disc bounced off a tree and flew back into Alex's head, we all busted a gut laughing. Michael was good at disc golf, had his own special discs and everything. He gave me a few pointers:

"See your disc landing in the basket before you throw it."

"Keep your hand flat, parallel to the ground."

"It's not about your force, it's about your focus."

We had a good time together out there in the woods that day, it smelled good out there too. Like trees and earth and damp leaves. It smelled *alive*. I remember thinking I should do things like that more often.

Afterwards, I suggested doing some blow and going to the strippers. They both looked at me like I had three eyes, which made me regret asking them. But I didn't want to go home yet, and it's sort of pathetic going to the strippers by yourself.

"What the hell? It's Saturday night," Michael said. So we got in the Jeep and did some bumps on the way downtown. But it was sort of awkward once we got there. It was like they'd never been to a strip club before. They didn't know where to look. They didn't know what to say. They didn't know what to do. They didn't even want to play the loonie game. We just had one pitcher between us, so we didn't stay very long.

"See her tattoo?" I nodded to the chick on stage. She had a playboy bunny silhouette on her hip.

"Yeah," Michael said.

"I did that."

"Really?"

I nodded.

It wasn't true, but it could've been. And at least it started a conversation. They asked me all about my apprenticeship and my shop and what was the craziest thing I had ever tattooed and what do I think about their tattoos and all the usual annoying questions that people ask when they find out I'm a tattoo artist.

But it was good.

....

One day Michael borrowed a longboard, said his was stolen recently, and we went out and bombed hills for the afternoon. God, that was good times. I hadn't skated with anyone since I'd left Calgary. And I had missed it. We were getting up some real speed that day too. A *Check Your Speed* sign clocked me doing sixty-nine coming down the hill at the top of Yates. I was weebling and wobbling like a motherfucker, but I did not fall down.

Michael liked to drink too, so we had a couple nights on the town. He took me to a party once on Haultain. It was at this huge black-and-white mansion with forty-seven rooms or something insane like that. I didn't know the party was going to be a zombie theme. Everyone was dressed up, and there were probly six hundred people there. It was a trip. Michael and I were really stoned and all the zombies running around were freaking me out. I didn't know anyone else there, and Michael had disappeared upstairs with some freaky zombie bride. So I cut out early, took my beer, plus a couple more from the fridge that would never be missed, skated home, rolled a joint, and cracked a beer. Sometimes I just don't feel like being around people. Most people are idiots, and if you're gonna be around them, you have to really want to. You have to have the patience.

....

I was partying pretty much all the time by then, just killing time until I could re-open. I was still drawing, though not as much. I guess the coke made me too agitated to sit still long enough to draw anything decent.

Michael liked coke, but he wasn't crazy about it. He was mainly a pothead and that was alright by me. Potheads you can trust, at least. They don't have the same greedy grabby neediness that other druggies get. I was doing a lotta coke with Kate, or alone. I was also smoking heroin most nights, usually just a little tiny hit around bedtime to help me get to sleep.

············

Kate really wanted to try heroin but I wasn't hot on the idea. I didn't want her hooked on coke *and* junk. One drug addiction was enough. I denied her for a long time, but she kept bringing it up. One night she came over and we had a few joints and some beers and listened to Pink Floyd's *Dark Side of the Moon* and watched *The Wizard of Oz* on mute on Kate's portable DVD player. It was trippy shit, man. When the movie was over we had sex. Afterwards, Kate cried. I've heard that women sometimes cry after a fantastic orgasm and that's normal, so I didn't worry about it. I reached for my cigarettes and lit one.

"I still think about that night all the time, Ant."

"Don't. He was alright."

"How do you know?"

"We would've heard about it if he'd died."

She buried her head in my chest and I smoothed her hair over and over while her hot tears dripped down my belly.

"Shh, it's okay, don't cry." I kissed the crown of her head.

I guess I thought it would cheer her up or get her mind off it, so I suggested chasing the dragon. Kate was keen so I got out the tinfoil. We smoked heroin in bed together, and for the millionth time, I wished she was sleeping over. But she couldn't. She stayed for another hour or two and we just chilled in bed, she said she felt very relaxed and peaceful and really comfortable. She said nothing hurt anymore.

"I want you to give me a tattoo," she said.

"Right now?"

"No," she giggled.

"What do you want?"

"Something beautiful," she murmured, and slipped her hand inside of mine.

We stared at the ceiling for a while. I thought of birds and flowers and waves and spirals and planets in brilliant colours. I don't know what Kate thought of. She got up off the futon and put her jeans on. I stared at her breasts. They were beautiful breasts. She put on her black bra, then pulled a black hoodie over her head. She grabbed her purse.

"Hey, are you okay to drive?"

"Yeah, I'm fine," she said. "I just feel tired, that's all."

"You sure?"

"Yeah." She leaned down and kissed my lips. "Don't worry."

"Are you sure, Kate? You can stay."

"Bye," she said, and walked out the door.

....

I fell into a dreamy lucid state. My body disintegrated into my futon, and everything was totally and completely relaxed, soon I was asleep. I woke up to the sound of sirens hollering past my open window. I felt a sharp pang in my gut. I wanted to call Kate and make sure she got home safely, but I knew it was too late to be calling her with him there. I'd just see her at the bagel shop in the morning. We could have a wake and bake. I went back to sleep, thinking about licking cream cheese off her naked body.

....

In the morning I felt real cloudy headed so I had a little line to wake me up. Hey, it works faster than coffee. Then I wandered down to the bagel shop, but it wasn't open yet. Again I had a bad feeling, but I figured Kate had probly slept in or something and I decided to call her later. I walked downtown and got breakfast. The eggs were slimy and the toast was cold but the waitress was semi-hot, and flashed me a nipple, so it wasn't a total loss. After I paid, I called Kate's phone but there was no answer. I walked and walked without really thinking about where I was going. I ended up out at Mile Zero. I smoked three cigarettes and stared at the ocean and the mountains and felt small.

The next day I went to the bagel shop first thing and there was another chick there, a chick I'd never seen before. She had red hair and glasses and was flatter than Saskatchewan.

"Where's Kate?"

"Who's Kate?"

"Kate who works here."

"Oh my God! I think she got in a car accident or something. She's in Jubilee."

....

I ran out the door and all the way to the hospital. I was so out of breath when I got there I couldn't talk, I was gasping Kate's name to the lady at reception. I probly looked hysterical.

"There's no one on my list by that name," she said.

"Kate!"

"No."

"Kate Swan!"

"Sorry."

"Kathryn! Kathryn Swan!"

....

I wasn't allowed to see her, even though I practically begged on my knees. The lady behind the desk was a useless cunt. She told me nothing except that Kate was not allowed visitors outside of immediate family. I was freaking out, man. I flipped. I got in her face. "Listen, lady, it's not like I don't give a fuck what you're saying, but I don't give a fuck what you're saying. I'm going in there. That's all there is to it. NOW TELL ME WHICH ROOM SHE'S IN!" And then two security guys gripped my shoulders and hustled me out the door. But I was too upset to be embarrassed. I could feel my lips, my whole body, trembling with anger. I wanted to throw a huge rock through those sliding glass doors and see if they would let me in then. I looked around for a rock for a while, but then I gave up and smoked a cigarette and simmered down a bit.

Later that night I called the hospital to find out how she was doing. It was a different receptionist, I could tell. She had a kind voice. I told her I was Kate's boyfriend.

"Oh, yes, hello. I believe we met yesterday."

"No. This is her other boyfriend."

"Oh, I see."

And I could tell by her voice she understood exactly what was going on, but she wasn't going to judge me. She was just going to tell me what I never wanted to hear: that Kate had fallen asleep at the wheel two nights ago, slammed into an arbutus and totalled her Civic. She had suffered massive internal injuries and severed her brain stem.

....

I could hardly believe what I was hearing. My whole body started to convulse and I had to hang up the phone so I could go dry heave over the sink. The word "vegetable" popped into my head and I hated myself for thinking that. Kate was not a vegetable. She was a human being. She was my best friend.

....

I blame myself entirely for what happened to Kate. It should've been me.

....

I called the hospital every day to find out when I could see her and, finally, on the third day, she was moved out of the ICU and I was allowed. I was nervous about running into her parents or her boyfriend, but mostly I was nervous about seeing her, seeing her like that, knowing that she would never be the same Kate again. I smoked a joint before I left, just to calm my nerves.

I asked at reception if anyone was visiting her right now, and there wasn't, so that was a relief. I found her room, room 213, took a deep breath, and went inside.

....

There were two big bouquets of lilies in her room, and the smell was so strong I nearly gagged. Kate looked like a little alien all shrivelled up in her bed and pale pale pale. She didn't even look like Kate. I guess she wasn't really Kate anymore. Well, she was and she wasn't.

I pulled a chair up beside the bed and stared at her. Everything in me was telling me to leave, to get the hell out of there, but I made myself stay. I forced myself to sit down and look at her. Really look at her.

She had wires stuck all over her arms and tubes up her nose, a machine was breathing for her. It was loud and reminded me of an accordion. Some of her hair was stuck to her forehead. She had two black eyes and probly a broken nose. There were stitches in her top lip. I wasn't sure if she was sleeping or unconscious or in a coma or what, and there was no one around to ask. I reached over and took her hand. It was soft like always, but it felt cold and papery.

"I'm sorry, Kate. I am so, so sorry." Then I hung my head in my hands and began to cry.

....

The next morning I woke up, did a line, had a shower, then went to see Kate. But when I walked into her room, he was there, standing in the corner with his arms folded across his chest like he was waiting for something.

"Who the fuck are you?" He was short with a shaved head, but pure muscle, like a pit bull. It had never occurred to me that he would be short. He was probly the same height as her, maybe even an inch or two shorter.

"Just a friend of Kate's." I propped my skateboard against

the wall, turned to look at Kate on the bed, hooked to her breathing machines, IVs, heart monitor. She looked the same as yesterday, all the colour gone from her face. Then I felt his eyes on me.

"You're the dealer. The tattooist."

I nodded.

He sat down in a chair and rubbed his palms together. "Man, I could really use your help today," he said.

I went and stood beside Kate. My strong, spunky, sexy Kate. I wanted to touch her face, to hold her hand. But I couldn't. Not with him there. I wished he would leave. I stared down at her, watched closely to see if her eyes would flutter open like in the movies. I waited. They didn't open.

The air felt thick, heavy. It reeked of the lilies. My head hurt. It felt like it was full of sand. He coughed. I wondered if he knew and, if he did, would he kill me?

"Do you wanna go grab a beer or something?" His knees jiggled up and down. He put his hand into his mouth, gnawed on his fingernails. He was jonesing. I watched Kate's chest rise and fall beneath the green sheet. Here she was, in a coma, on her death bed for fuck's sake, and all he wanted to do was go out and get high. He was pathetic. I almost felt sorry for the guy.

"Yeah, okay. Just give me a minute."

"Sure, no problem." He stood and shifted his weight from foot to foot, scratched his armpit.

I closed my eyes. I spoke to Kate in my head. I told her I was sorry and that she wasn't allowed to die. I told her that somehow I would find a way to make it up to her, to make everything alright again. I told her everything was going to be okay. I told her I would give her the tattoo she wanted once she was out of the hospital, and it would be the most beautiful tattoo in the universe, because it would be on her. I told her to hold on.

....

He drove a black Honda CRX with shiny rims and a ridiculously oversized spoiler. Snoop Dogg boomed from his subwoofers. We made a quick stop at my place. I made him wait in the car. I got him an eight ball and a QP of weed. I threw in a little extra bud because, let's face it, he was gonna need it. He paid and let me keep the change, then we each did a couple bumps and went to the George & Dragon.

Carmen was working. "Who's your friend, Ant?"

"Bradley," he said, and stuck out his hand. His fingers were short and stubby. The way he looked at Carmen made me feel sick.

"Pleasure to meet you," she said.

"Likewise." He grinned. He was flirting with Carmen while Kate lay dying in a hospital bed a kilometre away. I wanted to kill him.

When Carmen left us he leaned across the table, lowered his voice, "They found heroin in her bloodstream."

I raised my eyebrows, said nothing.

"She never would've touched that shit, man. I know she wouldn't have. She probly thought she was doing coke." His grey eyes widened. "You don't . . . do you?"

"No, no. Just the basics."

"Good, that's good. Yeah, she probably got it off one of her girlfriends, dumb bitches, all of them."

My stomach was making loud noises and I hoped he couldn't hear it.

"So, tattoos, eh?"

"Yeah."

"That's pretty cool. I got a couple myself."

"Oh yeah?" Like I gave a fuck.

He pulled up his sleeve and showed me the ugly pot leaf on his shoulder. Below, it said *4:20 4-Life*. *What a fuckin heat bag*, I thought. *Get me away from this asshole.* He finished his beer and let out a loud belch, signalled to Carmen to bring us two more.

I was drinking Guinness because that's what I ordered when I was hungry. It's like a meal in a glass. It even has vitamins and iron and shit in it. I was staring into my glass, admiring the creamy head, when he said, "I cheated on her."

I took a long drink, totally non-committal. I set the glass down, swallowed.

"A lot." He scrunched his face up.

I nodded.

"I'm a terrible person, I know I am. I deserve to rot in hell. I don't even know why I did it. She's a good lay, you know."

I knew.

"She's great. It's just that after three, four years with the same person, well, you start wanting to sample a few more flavours from the dessert tray. Know what I mean?"

"Yeah." Why the fuck was he telling me this? He didn't even know me. And I was Kate's friend, not his.

"You have a girlfriend?"

"No, not right now."

"Yeah, it's hard with women, being in your line of work, you never know if she's using you or if she actually likes you. I've been there, man."

I nodded.

"Do you think I should tell her?"

I shrugged.

"I just feel like I have to get it off my chest, you know? If she . . . then at least I would've come clean."

"Would you want her to tell you if it were the other way around?"

"Fuck no, I'd kill her."

"Hm."

"But it's not the other way around. It's this way around."

"Well then, I guess you gotta do what you gotta do." I finished my beer. I couldn't see it making much difference at this point. Kate's brain stem was severed. I doubted that she'd be hurt by his confession. She probly already knew anyways, she wasn't a total dumbass like him.

"I have to go." He put a twenty down on the table. "Thanks for everything, eh? You're a lifesaver." Then he pushed through the door.

Carmen delivered my nachos and sat down across from me and helped herself to a couple. "Who was that guy?"

"Just some dirtbag I never want to see again," I said.

"Yummy." She watched him through the window.

"Aren't you dating Andrew?"

"We're on a break."

"No shit, eh? You know, I'm not a dirtbag."

"Yes you are!" She hit me in the chest. "You're worse than a dirtbag. You're a scumbag!"

I looked down at my chest and rubbed the spot she'd hit, I stuck out my bottom lip.

"Having another, cry baby?" She picked up my glass.

"Okay."

....

I went to the strippers that night. Why? Because going to a strip club is like entering an alternate universe, an alternate reality. The lights, the music, the girls—none of it is real. That's why it's so comforting. Because you know that no matter what kinda fucked up shit is going on in your life, you can go to the strippers and everything will be predictable, everything will be exactly the same. The girls will dance and take off their clothes and the men will give them money. It's straightforward. It's easy. You don't have to think. You can just watch. So that's what I did. It took my mind off Kate for a while, and that's why I was there. But I did something I'm not proud of. I paid for a blow job. I don't know why I did it. I guess I thought it would make me feel better. Like a little treat.

It was a platinum blonde stripper I'd seen a few times before. Her stage name was Sally Paradise. She was a strong dancer and did a lotta creative stuff with the poles. She took me into the dingy room in the back where a guy the size of a rhinoceros stood, standing guard. She drew a little black curtain between us and rhino man and started unzipping my jeans. She wore a pink terry cloth dress that fell to her knees. It was cut low to expose her ballooning cleavage. I tried to touch her breasts to find out if they were real but she slapped my hand away. Her mouth was wet and her tongue was quick and she knew exactly what to do to get me off as fast as possible. We were in there maybe two, three minutes before she handed me a plastic cup to unload into. It cost $35.

···········

That night I dreamt that Kate and her boyfriend had traded places and it was him in that hospital bed and her out snorting coke and drinking beer with me. Kate and I snuck into the hospital in the middle of the night and pulled out all his life support. Then we went to the George & Dragon and it was empty. Kate took me behind the bar and gave me a blow job and then we drank everything behind the bar that we wanted and went into the kitchen and made ourselves cheeseburgers and fries. I had to wash all the dishes and mop the floors. Kate told me she loved me and I told her the same. Then we curled up in one of the booths together and fell asleep.

···········

The next afternoon I went to see Kate, and her parents were in the room when I walked in.

"Oh, sorry," I said and started to shut the door.

"It's okay, come in," her mom said. She was short with dark hair like Kate's, and her dad was big all over and had dimples. He looked like the kinda guy who could be jolly, under normal circumstances.

"Are you a friend of Kathryn's?" her dad asked.

"Yeah, I'm Anthony." I shook his hand. His grip was strong and hard. I took her mom's hand, it was soft and limp and full of sparkly rings. "Nice to meet you," I said.

"And you." She had navy half-circles beneath her eyes. She probly hadn't slept in days.

All three of us turned to look at Kate. It was awkward being in there with them and seeing the pain in their eyes. The pain I had caused. I wanted to leave.

"How did you know Kathryn?" Her mom asked.

"I met her at the bagel shop where she worked. Works."

Her mom nodded, not taking her eyes off her daughter.

"Were you with her the night of her accident?" her dad asked.

"No."

"No one seems to know where she was coming from." Her

113

prick

mom had a hoarse voice. "Bradley said she had gone out for drinks with her girlfriends, but they were all questioned and none of them saw her or heard from her that night."

"I don't know."

"The police might want to talk to you anyway, you should leave us your number, just in case," her dad said.

"Sure, no problem." There was a notepad on the table with the disgusting lilies. I tore off a sheet and wrote a fake number on it and handed it to her dad.

"Thanks." He folded it in two and put it in his breast pocket, never taking his eyes off me.

"Well, I should get going," I said, and stepped backwards towards the door. I looked at Kate once more and silently said goodbye to her.

"You can stay, if you want," her mom said.

"I can't."

"We don't mind."

"I can't."

....

I went home and heated up a can of chicken noodle soup. Grace used to say that chicken noodle soup always makes you feel better, no matter what. I guess this time was an exception.

....

I didn't go to the hospital again because I didn't want to deal with the pigs. I had enough to worry about without being interrogated. I just laid low for a few days and didn't leave the house except to make deliveries. Sometimes, for a minute or two, I kinda forgot about what had happened to Kate. I know that sounds terrible. Maybe I was in denial, I don't know. I kept thinking she was gonna walk into my shop and bring me an everything bagel with cream cheese, or that she would call and get me to bring over an eight ball. I know it's crazy, but I just wanted to see her again, how she really was, one last time. I thought maybe she would make a miraculous recovery and realize that her boyfriend was an asshole and she should really be with me. I thought maybe I could help with her rehab and nurse her back to health. And things would go back to how they were before, only they'd be way better, because Kate would be *my* girlfriend. I tried to put the whole thing out of my head for a few days, so I drank and did a lotta drugs and listened to a lotta music. Music I knew Kate liked: Pixies, Sublime, Nirvana. I sent her telepathic messages to stay strong, that I loved her and would wait for her.

I prayed. I prayed that she would be okay. It felt strange and stupid to be praying again after so many years. I felt like a fraud, but I did it anyways. I didn't know what else to do.

....

I called the hospital six days later, to see how she was doing. The nice receptionist answered. She told me that Kate's parents had decided to take her off life support, and she had passed away last night.

"What?"

"I'm sorry, sir."

"But, they didn't even ask me."

"I'm sure it was a very difficult decision."

"What if she had gotten better?" I was yelling into the phone but I didn't care.

"She never would have been the same, you have to understand." She sighed.

"Miss Swan suffered severe brain damage. She would have been permanently paralyzed, she would never have been able to take care of herself, she wouldn't have been able to communicate, she wouldn't have even been aware of you being in the same room with her."

"But she was alive! She was *alive!*"

"If you'd like to come in and talk to someone we can arrange that."

"No, I don't want to talk to anyone. I just . . . I just can't believe they did that. I can't believe she's gone."

"I'm sorry for your loss," she said.

It hurt to breathe and my chest felt like I'd been stabbed.

"Goodbye." The line went dead, and everything in me fell apart.

....

Later, I found out that her parents had Kate's body flown to Kelowna to have the funeral, since that's where all her family was and that's where she grew up. I thought about going. I figured it would take two days to take the ferry over to Vancouver and hitchhike through the Okanagan. No way in hell was I getting back on the Greyhound. I knew if I went to her funeral, then I could pay my proper respects. I could say goodbye. I could tell her what I never could when she was alive, that I loved her and always would. I could see her one last time. And that's what really got to me, that's what really hurt. If I didn't go to Kelowna, I would never ever ever ever ever see her again. And I didn't think I could live with that. I didn't even have a picture of her.

So I packed a bag for Kelowna. I was in line for the number 72 bus that goes to the Schwartz Bay ferry terminal. It was a double decker bus and I was planning to sit on the top deck in the very front, so that I could have that whole expansive view in front of me. A clear view of what was ahead. I got on the bus and bought my ticket and climbed up the narrow-ass staircase. Both the front seats were full. And I thought, *This isn't right.* This isn't the way it's supposed to go. So I squeezed back down the stairs and went out the back door of the bus. I didn't even ask the driver for my money back or anything. I don't know why. I just changed my mind at the last second, I blew it off. I had a bunch of reasons why I shouldn't go and none of them were very good, but they were my own reasons.

....

I hid away in my shop for a long while after Kate passed away. I didn't answer the cellphone, I didn't make deals or deliveries. I still had a huge supply of drugs that I had picked up off Michael, before Kate .

. . but I wasn't up to interacting with customers. I didn't want to see anyone, talk to anyone, look at anyone. I ate Kraft Dinner and Mr. Noodles and toast. I couldn't eat bagels without crying.

I put on a toque and shades and went to the drugstore. I bought a syringe and cotton balls, a carton of cigarettes, a pack of lighters, a ginger ale, and a Mars bar. I had decided to shoot heroin. Try anything twice right? I wasn't afraid of needles, so I guess I was either gonna be a tattoo artist or a junky.

....

I cooked up a little bit of fine white powder and water on a spoon, the way I'd seen Jesse and so many others do. It boiled to a liquidy amber and I filled up my syringe, using a cotton filter as I'd been shown. Then I held up the needle and flicked at it to get the bubbles out. You have to get the bubbles out or else they get into your bloodstream and make your heart explode. It would be ironic to go out that way really, because it wouldn't be the heroin or the rock and roll lifestyle that killed you, it would be a teensy tiny little air bubble. I can see the headline now:

Bubble Kills Man

Tragic. I wrapped a belt around my arm. It was the only belt I owned, and it had belonged to Seth. I tightened it up and poked at a greenish vein. I took a sharp breath as I watched my own blood, the colour of tea, bloom into the syringe. Then I slowly pressed the plunger down, filling myself with God's own medicine.

A warm tingling at the base of my skull and then the top of my scalp opened up and the stars rushed in. Everything was brighter and clearer and smoother and better than ever before. Total relaxation and a sublime euphoria overtook me. For a moment I felt nauseous, but it was not unpleasant. It passed quickly. I stretched out on my bed and breathed in the goodness and glory of a true heroin high. This was it. This was the feeling I'd been waiting twenty-one years for.

....

I hibernated in the cool dark cave of my shop and tied off every six or seven hours. I smoked weed, drank beer, listened to the radio, and tried not to think. About anything. I drew a lot and some of my drawings scared me. Sometimes I would see something I'd done the day before and wonder who drew it and how it got there. When I was high I could draw for five or six hours at a time. I could completely lose myself in it. And this was soothing for me. It was a release.

I went through a lotta dope that I was supposed to be selling and this made me very anxious while I was cooking up, but as soon as I was high, I didn't give a fuck. Whenever I got worried about it, I just got high again, and then I didn't care, I didn't fucking give a fuck about anyfuckingthing at all. Money doesn't matter when you're doing heroin. Having Lucifer's Choice on your ass doesn't matter when you're doing heroin. Being lonely doesn't matter, having sex doesn't matter, food doesn't even matter. Fuck all matters when you're doing heroin. The only thing that matters is heroin. Nothing in the world can hurt you. Nothing can touch you. You're safe.

....

Heroin is probly the best friend you can have at a time like that, and I was glad for it. And glad for my easy access to so much of it. I didn't care that I would have to find thousands of dollars to pay LC for it, I just kept doing it and everything was fine. I knew I would have to pay for it, all of it, at street cost, and I was fine with that. I knew I would run out sooner or later and that I would have to kick it and get shittingshits sick, and I was fine with that. As long as I could stay high for the foreseeable future, everything was fine.

The thing about being high on heroin is that everything slows right down. For some reason, the world is a lot easier to handle in slow motion. I don't know why, exactly. It's like you can get a little bit of control back in your life because you can hold the day down and watch it crawl by. You don't have to race to keep up with it all anymore. You can sort of freeze time. You can stop it and start it up again whenever you want. You can't rewind and you can't fast forward, but you can pause. You can go frame by frame.

So, like I said, I was high all the time and I didn't give a solid fuck about anything. Time passed so slowly that it became meaningless. The past didn't matter. The future didn't matter. I was only living in the present, where everything was cool, everything was fine, everything was sweet. Finally, I could relax. Every day was predictable and identical, and that was comforting. No surprises. I had a routine: I would wake up, shoot up, have a cigarette, get coffee, have some toast, have a shower, shave, draw for a few hours, have another bang, nod off for a while, not think, not care, just be, smoke a joint around 4:20, maybe do some push ups and sit ups while I listened to the radio, draw some more, eat something, fix again and chill for a bit, then get into bed and float away.

This day repeated itself again and again for well over a month. But I'd lost track of days so I'm not sure exactly how long it was. I knew I'd have to stop when I ran out of dope. I accepted that. I was getting close to the bottom and only had a few bags left, but I wasn't too worried. I kept up my routine, using almost exactly the same amount of powder each time I cooked up. I knew that I could handle that amount and that it was good, and even though I was curious about what more would feel like, I was paranoid about ODing. Probly because, like everyone else, I'd been brainwashed by Hollywood. But I didn't want to be found cold and blue in a bathtub like all the rest of those fuckin junky rock stars. But obviously, I wouldn't be, because I didn't even have a bathtub.

....

One night, I was lying in bed after just shooting up and I heard this heavy pounding on my door. I figured it was Hank looking for his money, he'd knocked before and I hadn't answered and he'd eventually gone away. I didn't move. I didn't intend to move. I looked at my ceiling. I loved my ceiling. Suddenly, there was an explosion so loud I thought it had burst my eardrums. I was scared shitless. I grabbed my kit and jumped into my closet. *Holy fuck holy fuck what the fuck is this?* I sat down on a bucket, my knees knocking together. All I could smell was the dirty mop in my face as I strained to hear what was going on over the ringing in my ears. I heard the cash register open, there was about $300 in there. I could hear someone, maybe two people, stomping and banging around, fucking with my shit, overturning chairs. And then something smashed. And then another deafening explosion followed by a sharp crackle, and I realized it was a gunshot and I thought, *Fuck, this is for real. This is the LC come to execute me.* I didn't know what to do. I looked up. I stood on the overturned bucket and pulled down the trap door to the attic. The hinges groaned. I climbed the three rotten rungs of the ladder, heaved myself up, and tried to quietly shut the attic door. I could still hear them down there and hoped to hell that they hadn't heard me. Then they were in my back room, my bedroom. My ears felt like they were full of cotton. I heard my futon being flipped over. I kept my porn underneath it, and about a hundred bucks. I heard someone laugh. A scratchy, gravelly laugh. I huddled in a ball, trying not to breathe, and listened while they searched my room: for drugs, for money, for me. I've never been so scared in my life. The closet opened with a bang and they pushed some things around in there. I was terrified that they would open the attic door and come up to investigate. And then I would be killed. But first I would be tortured. Oh God, I had to sneeze. I had to sneeze and I was going to be tortured and killed when I did. I held my breath and plugged my nose. They stopped moving for a few seconds, they were quiet. They were listening. Then one of them said, "Let's go, he ain't here." And they walked out. I heard their boots clomping all the way to the front door, and when I didn't hear their boots anymore, I let out what was probly the loudest sneeze of my life.

And then I started crying.

I sat up in the attic crying and sneezing for probly half an hour.

I couldn't stop shaking and I couldn't stop crying and I couldn't stop sneezing and I was freezing cold and my nose was pouring snot all over the place and I didn't care. All I could do was sit up there thinking how I nearly just got offed and how that was pretty fucked up.

Finally, I calmed down enough to open the trap door and

climb down. My mattress money was gone, but my room was in no more of a mess than it had been. I walked out into the main part of my shop. What I saw there, hurt me. My skull ashtray was smashed on the floor and there were ashes and cigarettes everywhere, the coffee table had been kicked over and broken, the chairs were flipped upside down, the cash register was empty, and my big floor to ceiling centre mirror panel was shattered. Spidery cracks spread out from a bullet hole in the centre. I looked at the mirror and saw myself reflected in the dark, fragmented pieces. My eyes were huge and frightened, my head was bulbous, my arms were sticks, my hands were massive, and my body looked long and warped. I laughed a sharp little laugh, maybe from relief, or maybe because I reminded myself of a creature you'd see in a Dr. Seuss book. I shook my head because I'd paid nearly $900 for that mirror. And now it was worthless.

Well, honey, Grace's voice rang in my head, *you can't expect your actions not to have consequences.*

She'd said that to me when I got expelled and had to go to AADAC. And here I was again, almost ten years later, still getting in shit over dealing dope.

Well, I had no one to blame but myself. I should've seen it coming, and I was lucky it wasn't any worse than it was. Because, let's face it, it could've been a whole lot worse. I'm such a fucking idiot sometimes. I should've told Hank and Michael what happened and that I was taking a break for a while. There was no way they could have known about Kate. Of course Lucifer's Choice assumed the worst when I'd gone AWOL. I don't know what I was thinking. I guess I wasn't. I was just dealing with too much right then to have to deal with my supplier and whoever else needed to know my whereabouts, but I was stupid not to. *Really fucking stupid business move right there, Ant.* I lit a cigarette and kept watching myself in the ruined mirror while I smoked it.

Oh well, what's done is done, I thought. Then I turned the chairs and coffee table upright, got out my works, sat down, and had another bang.

....

When I woke up in the morning, I was hit by this massive wave of relief. I thought: *It was only a nightmare, it didn't happen. It was only a dream! Thank God! None of that actually happened! Everything's fine! Kate's alive! I'm alive! I'm going to see her! I'm going to have a bagel and coffee with her!* And I stood up from the chair and saw the mirror, and then it all came crashing down on me. Literally. The broken shards of mirror chose that moment to fall out onto the floor.

....

I wanted so much to live without regret, to live without guilt, to live without shame. But I couldn't seem to erase any of it. Undo any of it. Or forget any of it. Heroin didn't change that. I still had to live with myself every minute of every day. The world went on. Time didn't stop. And the people I loved stayed dead.

....

I stood out front of my shop and smoked a cigarette. It had just stopped raining and the sun was going down, the clouds looked like cotton candy, and there was a brilliant double rainbow ripping up the sky in front of me with all its happy, shiny colours. And I knew it was beautiful, but I couldn't feel anything.

That night I used the last of the heroin I'd been given to sell. I was already thinking about where I could go in the morning to get more.

....

The next day was clear, sunny blue. I could hear the birds chirping outside my shop and even though I felt sort of shitty, I went for a walk and forced myself to look into the eyes of people I passed on the street. I saw eyes full of fear and sadness and anger. I saw eyes full of hatred and pain. I walked up to Willow's Beach, lay down, and buried myself in the sand. I looked up at the giant willow tree above me, gently waving in the breeze. The ocean was a shimmery aquamarine, kids were laughing and building sandcastles, and dogs were swimming and barking and fetching sticks. This little kid didn't see me buried in the sand and he stepped on my arm and I said "Ouch!" and he started laughing hysterically. He laughed so hard he fell down in the sand and then dug a little hole and buried himself beside me and we stayed like that for a long time. Neither of us said anything. We looked over at each other once in a while and smiled like we shared a secret. His eyes were shiny and brown and filled with delight. Eventually, his parents started looking for him and calling his name. He got up and brushed himself off. "Bye!" he said, and ran away.

....

I stayed in my hole in the sand for a very long time and I decided that I'd had enough heroin for a while and I'd better face reality again before I lost it completely. I owed Lucifer's Choice about seven grand and I had no fucking idea how I was going to get it. I went home and put away my works and prepared to sell the rest of the shit I had: a bit of coke and some weed. I turned the cellphone on and listened to the messages. There were forty-two messages and probly would have been more but the mailbox was full. I returned calls to those who wanted what I still had. I knew that I had to get out and make some fast cash today, because tomorrow, and the next couple days, I was going to be really, really sick.

....

The next few days were pretty fuckin rough, but I knew that I deserved to feel like shit, so I was fine with it. In fact, I sort of wish it had been worse than it was. It was just like a really nasty super flu, but it wasn't as horrible as I had expected it to be. Yeah, I was farting butterscotch and, yeah, I threw up every time I stood up, and my hair hurt and my eyes burned and my skin crawled and I wanted to tear my skin off and my legs cramped and jerked and I hurt all over and I shivered all the time and I cried and I wanted to die and I wanted more heroin more heroin more heroin more. But still, it didn't feel like enough punishment.

But more than I wished that I had more heroin, I wished that I had someone there to take care of me and mop my forehead and bring me water and take my buckets away and rinse them out and bring them back and change my sheets and cover me with blankets and rub my back and hold me and tell me I was going to get through this. Tell me I was going to be okay. That everything would be okay.

....

Whoever said it takes three dopesick days to kick heroin must have been stoned. It takes a lot, lot longer than that. And every day is longer and sadder than you could have ever imagined. I don't know if it was the withdrawal or the depression or the guilt or the grief or the not eating properly or what, but I wanted to die in a terrible and violent way. I wanted to die that week more than I've ever wanted to do anything. I wanted to stop existing as the worthless bag of skin I am. It's a good thing I didn't have a gun in my shop or I would've put it in my mouth. I hated myself more than anyone has hated anything ever. I couldn't sleep, but all I wanted to do was sleep. I couldn't eat, but I needed something inside me. I needed something to fill me up. The only things I could keep down were chocolate milk and soda crackers. Every day it got a little less painful, a little bit easier. But I was beginning to realize that nothing would ever be easy again.

....

I called Hank.
        "Where in hell have you been?"
        "I fucked up, Hank."
        "Yeah, I got that."
        "I'm sorry."
        "As long as you're not a police informant, you may have a chance to redeem yourself."
        I explained to him what had happened to Kate, and then to me, and he said he was very sorry to hear that. He said he knew I'd figure something out and that if I could have the money in thirty days

there would be no penalty. He said I should've told him sooner, and asked me if I needed anything. I don't think he knew how much I appreciated that, or maybe he did, maybe he'd been there before. My throat started to close up and I thanked him and hung up. Hank was a friend and that was all I needed. I was grateful to have him on my side. I would get a line of credit or something and everything would sort itself out. Lucifer's Choice would spare me after all. I was so relieved I collapsed on my futon and slept deeply and uninterrupted for the first time in days.

....

When I was well enough, I gave myself a tattoo to remember Kate by. A chiaroscuro swan on my lower abdomen. It hurt more than any tattoo I've had before or since and I bled like a stuck pig. But I think she would have liked it. I think she would have thought it was beautiful.

....

I felt a little less worthless every day and eventually I was feeling sort of okay again. I thought maybe it was possible that I might actually survive this after all. Even though I missed Kate horribly, I sometimes forgot she was gone. It was easier for me to pretend that she had just gone away on a trip or moved to the mainland or something, and she wasn't coming back. When I pictured her six feet under, rotting in a box, worms eating out her golden eyes, that's when things got really hard. I tried to keep those thoughts out of my head. But I was just so lonely without her. Lonely, lonely, lonely and fucking lonely. That was my life, lonely.

....

I was looking forward to the re-opening of my shop in a few weeks, but I was still gonna deal on the side because the money was good, and money always comes in handy, especially when you owe LC seven large. Plus, it's nice to not have to pay for your own drugs. Michael had just gotten a shipment of premium cocaine in, and when I went over to pick up, we sampled a couple of lines to appreciate its superior quality. He asked me if I wanted to hang out for a bit, and I was grateful for that.

"Sorry to hear about your girlfriend, Ant."

"That's okay," I said. But it wasn't okay. It wasn't okay at all.

We smoked a fatty and played Grand Theft Auto for a while. Then we walked down to the cold beer and wine and got a couple six packs and ordered a pizza. It was good. I felt more normal than I had in a long time. Except that Michael's house was pimped out. Six bedrooms, leather furniture, bear skin rug, flat screen TV, massive sound system, turn tables, twelve-foot ceilings, marble flooring, a view of the ocean. Unbelievable. He had some fine art on his walls too, that one with the DJ spinning, and another one I recognized from somewhere, a man in an overcoat sitting on a chair but his chest is a birdcage and there's a bird inside. I don't know if they were originals or not, but they must have been worth something.

Alex, his roommate, was away a lot because his girlfriend lived in Vancouver, and I guessed that Michael probly got lonely once in awhile in all that space.

Michael told me he studied economics at UVic. I guess he was on the narcotics revenue scholarship. Well, it doesn't take a fucking university degree to figure out that you can never really get ahead in the straight world, doing a nine-to-five, sitting in front of a computer like some fuckin zombie for eight hours a day, wearing a tie and a nametag that says *Sucker*. That's no way to live, man. Surely, selling drugs would be better than that. Selling drugs was probly even a relatively safe business bet.

"Definitely a profitable venture," Michael said, looking around his house. "So far."

"Supply and demand, baby! Supply and motherfuckin demand."

....

I never asked Michael how he knew Hank. I assumed it was through getting tattooed. I could see that a couple of his tattoos were Hank's work.

Michael never mentioned where his weed came from and it always looked fresh and sticky, so I figured he had a grow-op somewhere in the house. I would've loved to have had a look at it, but it's not professional to ask about that sort of thing. Besides, if you know too much, you're a liability. The less you know, the better. That's been my experience, anyways.

....

We watched *Scarface*, which I hadn't seen since I was twelve or thirteen. I had liked it the first time I saw it, but I was too drunk and stoned to catch it all. This time, I could really appreciate it, and I decided that it was my new favourite movie. Fuck *A Clockwork Orange*. *Scarface* was the real deal.

I fell asleep on the leather couch and woke up later, cold and thirsty, to grey light leaking through the bay windows. Michael was stretched out on the other couch, snoring softly, his mouth hanging open. I threw a blanket at the end of the couch over him. I was out of smokes and his pack was sitting open on the coffee table so I took one out and slipped it behind my ear. Then I collected what I'd come for, put it in my bag, and quietly left.

....

Four days later I was next door getting a coffee and looked at the front page of the newspaper:

Twenty-one-year-old man beaten to death by golf club in Golden Oaks home

"What. The. Fuck." My breath whooshed out of me and I had to sit down. I held my head in my hands and read the entire article.

When I got to the end, I read it again. The words were swimming and the lines were blurring together and I felt dizzy and nauseous and sweaty and sick. I couldn't believe it. I didn't want to believe it. It was too much.

The victim's roommate arrived home to find him lying in a pool of blood. He was unable to make a positive identification because the body was beaten so badly that it was unrecognizable.

I felt a piercing pain in my chest. I wanted this to be a dream. I wanted it to be a lie. No, no, no, this was all wrong, this was a mistake. This was a joke. This couldn't happen. This wasn't happening. No fucking way was this happening. Not to Michael. Not to my buddy.

....

Michael was the first person to be murdered in that neighbourhood in over thirty years. Police were asking anyone with information to come forward. I wanted to help and I wanted the person who killed him to serve a life sentence with no possibility of parole. And not in fucking Club Fed William Head either, in a real jail where he would be properly punished. But I didn't have any information. I didn't know fuck all except that Michael sold drugs and his death was most likely drug related, which they'd probly already figured out. He might have owed someone a debt, but it sounded more like a robbery. I knew Lucifer's Choice had nothing to do with it because they weren't sloppy like that. This wasn't their style. And, besides, he was an associate of theirs, not a competitor or an enemy. Fuck, I hope they find whoever did it and find him fast before he gets to Mexico. If only I had been there, I could've helped him. I could've done something, you know? Fuck, I would've shoved that golf club so far up that guy's ass, it would've come out his mouth. I swear to God.

I sat there in the pizza shop staring at the newspaper and my vision filled with red. Michael was a good guy, a decent guy, he was a buddy of mine, and someone had killed him. Someone took his life away. But they didn't just shoot him, bang-bang. No. They fucking bludgeoned him with a fucking nine iron and beat the living shit out of him. Why would someone do that to Michael? Michael was nice! I didn't know him that well, but I *know* he didn't deserve that.

....

I went back to my shop and called Hank because I didn't know what else to do. He picked up on the first ring.

"Hank, what the fuck happened?"

"Ant?"

"Yeah, it's me."

"I don't know. We're working on it. We're working with the VPD, okay. We're gonna get this motherfucker."

"Fucking rights we are."

"Do you know anything?"

"I don't know."

"Well, do you or don't you?"

"No, no."

"Alright, then just stay low. The cops will probably want to talk to you because your number'll be on his phone."

"Okay."

"I'll be in touch," Hank said. Then he hung up.

....

Aw, fuck, fuck me, I was fucked. I wasn't supposed to be living in my shop, but I had nowhere else to go. I had way too many drugs on me and nowhere to hide them. I had to think. I needed a plan. I did a fat rail to clear my head. Then I paced around the shop and tried to think of what to do. I ate a power bar. I could hardly believe that Michael was dead. That he had been murdered. I could hardly believe what all had happened since I started dealing. I felt like bashing in a wall, I felt like crushing someone's skull, I felt like crying. But I couldn't. I punched a hole in my wall and recoiled in pain, sucking my knuckles. But it was necessary. I had to feel something. I put my hand under the tap and let the cold water run over it while it reddened and swelled. I wondered if it was broken, like everything else in my life.

Selling drugs is an evil thing. Everything about it is evil, from start to finish. If anyone ever tries to tell you different, they're probly on drugs. It's fucked. It fucks people up and it fucks people over. Forever. I knew that going in. I guess I've known it all along.

....

My nails were digging into the flesh of my hands so hard I started to bleed. That's when I realized: that cellphone wasn't even mine. Hank gave it to me. It was a Lucifer's Choice phone. It couldn't be traced to me. I had nothing to do with setting up that phone account. There was no way I'd be implicated, interviewed, interrogated, or otherwise. I laughed out loud and felt a warm rush of relief, but I was still pretty anxious. I wanted to get rid of the phone, get rid of my stash, I wanted out of the drug trade. For good.

....

For the next two days I worked like a dog and unloaded nearly five ounces of weed and about two ounces of coke. The little crumbs I had left I decided to keep for personal use. I took out my cut of the cash and went down to Capital Tattoo. Hank was there. We shook hands. I hadn't seen him since I'd collected from the Edmonton delivery. He looked tired. No one else was in the shop.

"Let's go into the back," I said.

He nodded and locked the front door and put the BACK IN FIVE MINUTES sign up. We went into the back room and he closed the door. My heart galloped like a racehorse. I could feel beads of sweat popping out on my forehead. I didn't know if I could do this, but I was going to do it anyways. I handed him an envelope full of cash and the cellphone. "I'm out," I said. "I'm done."

"Can't blame ya."

"Thanks for hooking me up with this gig and all, but I just want to tattoo now."

"Fair enough."

"I just want to make good tattoos for people and feel good about it." My voice cracked.

"I know."

ashley little

130

prick

It was too easy. "Can I...? Are you ... ?" I started to choke on the lump in my throat. "Is it really okay?"

"I'll have to make some excuses for you, but you should be alright. Long as you settle all your debts this month and keep your fuckin mouth shut."

I felt my face crumple against my will.

"Hey, kid, don't worry! It's not for everyone, right?" Hank stepped towards me and crushed me in a man-hug. He smelled like leather and smoke.

"I'm sorry," I sobbed into his vest.

He didn't say anything. He was squeezing me so hard I couldn't breathe. We stayed like that for a minute and I hoped there wouldn't be any snot on his vest, and then I backed away. "I gotta go," I said, and flew out the door.

....

I ran down to the breakwater. I don't know why I was running, I never run, I hate running. But, suddenly, I had to run as fast as I could. I ran to the end of the pier and had this overwhelming urge to hurl myself into that steel-blue water. I wanted to. I wanted to dive in and sink to the bottom and lie down on the ocean floor and never, ever have to come up again. But I knew it would be colder than a witch's tit in January down there and I didn't want to be cold anymore. I was tired of being cold all the time. I couldn't even remember the last time I felt hot. But I was warm from the run and I didn't want to ruin that. I caught my breath and wiped the tears and sweat off my face with my shirt and sat down at the end of the pier and dangled my legs over the water and lit a cigarette. I stayed there for a long time, just staring into the distance. The sky was battleship grey. I watched the waves, the silent purple mountains. I watched the ships and the seagulls float by. I didn't really think about anything. My mind was numb. Black clouds rolled in and started pissing rain. I was soaked within two minutes and freezing fucking cold, but the rain was somehow a relief.

I walked back to my shop with my head down and my hood up. I took a scalding hot shower then made some tea and toast. I felt a little better. Then I started thinking about Michael again. I knew that I would miss him. I already did. I wondered if I knew the guy who murdered him. I wondered what the guy was doing right now. And I wondered if he felt guilty.

....

The next morning I woke up to a violent pounding on the door of my shop. At first I thought I was dreaming, but then the pounding continued for a good minute or so. *What the hell is this?* I thought. *Someone wanting something real bad. Fuckin junkies. Well, they can fuck right off.* I put my pillow over my head.

"Victoria Police. Open up!"

Oh, fuck me. Here we go. I rolled over and grabbed the rest of my stash from underneath the futon, only a few little grains, and a couple buds. I calmly walked to the bathroom and flushed it all down the toilet. I washed my hands and pulled on a shirt and jeans. Then I went to the front door. I took a deep breath. I opened the door.

....

Two police officers stood in front of me. One male, one female. He was tall with a black moustache and she looked like a Latina supermodel. They had found my fingerprints at Michael's and wanted to question me. I rubbed my eyes and then I panicked for a split second. I was stuck inside a nightmare and couldn't wake up. But this wasn't a nightmare. This was my life. I looked at the ant on my forearm and I knew it was all real. Seeing my ant staring up at me made me feel better, like I could handle anything. Then I got my shit together and played it cool.

"Am I gonna need a lawyer?"

"No, this is just a routine questioning. You are not under arrest," Moustache said.

"Good."

I've always hated cops, but at least these two weren't total assholes.

I don't think I was ever a suspect. I think they just wanted information from me:

How did I know Michael?
Did he have any enemies?
Did he owe anyone money?
Did he owe me money?
Did he sell drugs?
Was he involved in illegal activities?
Who did he socialize with?
Who did he work for?
What was I doing at his house?
Did I golf?

I played it off like I'd only met him a couple times and had gone to his place to smoke a joint once. I told them I met him at the strippers and we got talking about tattoos. He said he was thinking of getting some new work done and wanted to talk to me about his design ideas. I didn't really know anything about him. Which was sort of true, I guess. Still, they kept pressing me. But I stuck to my story and they bought it.

At some point in my early teens, I'd become really good at lying. Especially to cops. I got the feeling they already had a prime suspect, but they were just covering their asses. They asked me why my shop had been closed for the last few months, and I rolled my eyes. Obviously, they knew why. It would be on my file. I told them anyways. I played along. They asked what I'd been doing for work while I'd been closed.

"Nothing. Living off my savings," I said.

"You must have an awful lot of savings. What's the rent on this place, fifteen, eighteen hundred a month?"

"Well, I'm a man of few needs."

Then they told me they had a warrant to search my shop.

"Let me see it," I said, all balls of big steel.

Moustache pulled something out of his ass. I looked at it, but I didn't see it. My mind was swimming and the words were so tiny. It looked like an official document though. I would have to let them search the shop. My mind was screaming at me that I was fucked Fucked FUCKED. But then a cold wave of clarity washed over me, and I realized that I had nothing. I had absolutely nothing on me. Not the drugs, not the scale, not the phone. Nothing. I was clean.

"Go ahead." I didn't give a flying fuck if they searched every square inch of my shop. I had nothing they could pin on me. Nothing they could use as evidence against me.

I don't know how I got away with it. Honestly, I don't know how I got away with half the shit I've done and why I'm not in jail right now. I really don't. I know I probly should be. I realize that. For some bizarre reason I was left untouched. I never got caught. For any of it. I don't know why.

I once met a guy whose brother went away for ten years for a crime that he didn't even commit. One day they tested his DNA and realized he wasn't the right guy and let him walk. Talk about a fair trial.

The cops didn't even ask me if I was living in my shop, which I was worried about getting in shit for the whole time. Maybe they knew I was living in there all along. They were efficient and quick in their search. They knew what they were looking for. I figured they were looking for a golf bag, or a weapon of some sort. Some evidence, bloody clothes, signs of a struggle, shit like that. I got a little nervous when Moustache went into the bathroom, but I figured what I'd flushed would already be on its way out to sea. Unless the toilet backed up, in which case, I was fucked. But they didn't find anything. There was nothing to find.

I stood by the door and smoked a cigarette while they went through my shit. I watched two fat seagulls pick out pizza crusts from the garbage can in front of my shop and inhale them like greedy little monsters.

....

The Latina supermodel cop gave me a nod on her way out the door. Moustache gave me a card with his number on it and told me to call him if I thought of anything. Anything at all. I wished the chick had given me *her* number. I said that I wished I knew more and I hoped they caught the guy who killed Michael. And I meant it. Moustache said they appreciated my cooperation. I don't think I'd ever do anything to help out a cop, smokin hot supermodel or otherwise, but I thought it was nice of old Moustache to say anyways. He said they'd be in touch and he said to take care. I always get a kick out of people saying that: "Take care." Take care of *what?*

....

For the rest of the week I went on a bender. Drinking and snorting and smoking all day. I just wanted to get obliterated and stay that way and forget everything.

All my life I've felt like I was walking a tightrope, on one side there's total chaos and on the other, normality, and that at any given time, I could fall either way. Last night, I fell. I fell and I fell and I fell and I'm sorry.

....

I had a few beers in me. I felt like being around people all of a sudden, so I had a nice little line and wandered downtown. I ended up at Lucky Bar. There was a band playing. A heavy rock band. I stood at the back with my beer and watched the show. People were dancing and getting right into it. I envied the guys on stage. They were good. I always wanted to play electric guitar, but I never learned how. I used to play drums in school, but I stopped after grade seven. Seth said it was a "good for nothing goddamn noisy racket." He stabbed holes in my drum kit one night, and I never played again.

Anyways, I had another beer and was feeling a little tipsy, so I went to the can to do a line. When I came out, Sonya was coming out of the ladies'. She was wearing these tight black leather pants and looked hotter than ever.

"Sonya?"

"Ant! How *are* you?" She gave me a big hug, which surprised me. But then I realized she was drunk.

I bought her a beer and we sat down at a little table near the door. She looked different. She looked happy.

"How's it going at Capital?"

"I'm not there anymore," she said, grinning.

"Uh oh, what happened?"

"No, no, nothing bad, don't worry, everything's cool. I'm moving to Vancouver. I'm opening my own studio. For women! All women tattoo artists and all women clients."

"No shit, eh?"

"No shit, man. I'm opening next month." She was swaying back and forth in her seat and smiling like mad.

"That's great, Sonya. I'm so happy for you." And I was. I really was. I excused myself and went to the bar and ordered us another round of beers and four shots of good tequila. I knew Sonya liked tequila, and this was a real reason to celebrate. When I got back to our table she was resting her head in her hands. I touched her bare shoulder. "Here's to you and your excess, I mean success." I handed her a shot and clinked my glass into hers. We threw them back and I put a lemon wedge in my mouth and sucked hard. I crossed my eyes and made a sour face and she laughed and laughed. And it was the most beautiful sound in the world. I insisted that the other two shots were for her.

"Ah, what the hell? It's my last night in Vic, I guess I might as well go out with a bang, eh?" She knocked them back.

She was going to leave without even saying goodbye to me. Oh, my heart hurt. If Sonya was gone, I would have nothing left. Absolutely fuck all. Nothing. Notafuckinthing, man. Nada.

"What's your shop gonna be called?"

"Shadow Ink."

I laughed. "Perfect."

"Do you want to dance?" She nodded her head towards the stage. The band was playing a cover of a cover of "I Will Survive" and I could not say no to her. Even though I hated dancing and was really bad at it and knew that I would make a total fool of myself, I could not say no.

....

I didn't realize how shitfaced she was until we went up front to dance and she was bumping into people and chairs. But we danced, we danced and, fucking hell, she was amazing. I couldn't stop staring at her ass in those leather pants. And then she started grinding with me, and shaking her tits in my face. It was too much. I couldn't stand it. I thought I was gonna explode. I ducked into the can and did another quick little line. Then went back to her. She was flinging her hair around like a fucking rock star. Her hair hit me in the face and it was all just too much.

When the next song ended I grabbed her hand and pulled her out the emergency exit to the back alley. I held her arms tight and shoved her up against the brick wall and kissed her hard on the mouth. Oh God, her mouth was so warm and soft and delicious. I wanted to crawl inside it. I just wanted her. Forever and ever and ever. She was all I'd ever wanted. And she was perfect. I started kissing her neck and unzipping those goddamn pants. She said three words: *Stop. No.* And *Don't.*

But I couldn't.

I just couldn't.

And then I was inside her.

And it was exactly where I had always wanted to be. For one, maybe two seconds, I knew pure and total bliss.

....

But then she brought her knee up hard and slammed me in the balls. I sank to the ground and she kicked me in the ribs and the stomach, again and again. She bootfucked me.

"You're a fucking asshole! You know that?"

"I know."

"Fucking pig!" She spat in my face and stumbled away, her boots clicking over the pavement.

"I'm sorry!" I yelled after her. "I'm sorry," I whispered.

....

I don't even know what I did. I don't. It happened so fast. I was so fucked up. I don't remember. I really don't know what happened. I didn't mean to hurt her. I just wanted her so bad, for so long. I thought she wanted me too. She wanted me though, I fuckin know she did. She wanted to know what a man felt like. Oh God, what did I do? I didn't think . . . I mean, I didn't want to . . . I can't believe I did that. I don't believe it. Oh God God God and Jesus in the sky. What have I done?

I don't know how long I was lying there, moaning in the filth of the alley. I wanted to dissolve into the pavement. I wanted to die.

....

Remembering becomes a difficult thing to do. Was there ever a time when I didn't fuck up everything I touched? Was there ever a time when I was good?

....

I fucked up. I know. I fucked up royally and now I'm so fucked. I just want to tattoo. That's all I've ever wanted to do. That's what I'm good at, that's what I love. Creating living, breathing skin pictures. Making art on human canvases.

I don't know what I'm going to do now. I know I should turn myself in, but what would be the point? So I can rot in some dank cell and get butt-raped every night for the next twenty-five years? Maybe I deserve that, I don't know.

Maybe I'll head south. Grow a beard. Get a tan. Yes, I am vain. Yes, I have lusted. For these and all the sins of my life, I am deeply sorry.

Glossary

AADAC Alberta Alcohol and Drug Addiction Centre
APBT American Pit Bull Terrier
AWOL Absent Without Leave
Baked stoned, high on marijuana
Bang dose of injected heroin *or* sexual intercourse
Blow cocaine
Brown heroin
Bud marijuana
Bumps small amounts of cocaine more convenient to snort than a line
Camel toe female genitalia, as seen through tight pants
CCR Credence Clearwater Revival
Chase the dragon smoke heroin by heating it through tinfoil and sucking up the vapours through a tube straw
Coco-puff marijuana cigarette laced with cocaine
Coke cocaine
Curb stomp to place someone's open mouth on a cement street curb and stomp on their head from behind, breaking teeth and possibly more
Doob, doobie marijuana cigarette
Dope heroin *or* marijuana
Dough money
Eight ball an eighth of an ounce of cocaine
Fatty large marijuana cigarette
Fixie a fixed gear bicycle
FTW Fuck The World *or* Forever Two Wheels
G&D The George and Dragon Restaurant and Pub
God's own heroin
GST Goods and Services Tax
H heroin
Heatbag/heatscore a person who attracts unwanted police attention
Holidays uneven areas in a tattoo where colour has lifted out during healing missed section of skin
Hoodie a hooded sweatshirt
Hundy hundred
ICU Intensive Care Unit
Isy isopropyl alcohol

IV intravenous
J joint, marijuana cigarette
JAFFO Just Another Fucker From Ontario
Junk heroin
Junky a drug addict, usually referring to a heroin addict but can also refer
    to addicts who consume other substances
Juvie juvenile detention centre
Kit drug kit
LC Lucifer's Choice Motorcycle Gang, a highly organized and very
    violent international crime syndicate dealing mainly in narcotics,
    weapons, and human trafficking, racketeering, and illegal gambling
    operations.
MF Motherfucker
OCAD Ontario College of Art and Design
OD overdose
OE Olde English; cheap beer with high alcohol content
O-zee ounce
Pigs/piggies police
Pinner tiny joint
Pot marijuana
PRD Pre-Rolled Doobie
Prez President of a criminal organization
Pro profile *or* professional
QP Quarter Pound
Rail line of cocaine
Rep reputation
Rotten Ronnie's McDonald's
Scratcher an unskilled tattooist practising unsafe methods
Speedball mixture of cocaine and heroin
TCB Taking Care of Business
THC Tetrahydrocannibinol, the main psychoactive ingredient in marijuana
The Wack Chilliwack, BC, Canada
TO Toronto, ON, Canada
Vic Victoria, BC, Canada
VPD Victoria Police Department
Wake and bake when smoking marijuana is the first activity upon waking
    up, before eating or showering
Weed marijuana
Works equipment used for injecting heroin: tourniquet, syringe, spoon, etc.

Acknowledgements

Thank you: my first reader, sounding board, and friend, Jonathan Parlee; Ben Parker for your honesty, astute observations, and not letting me make excuses; Randy Ingermanson for helping me finally get started; Amy Peelar and Darren Parnell for inspiring the original idea; my lovely editor, Shirarose Wilensky; the community of Ucluelet, BC, and the Clayoquot Writers Group for your encouragement and enthusiasm surrounding this novel. Thank you to my family for your unconditional love and support, and big-big thanks to my wonderful partner, Warren, for putting up with me, and keeping me fed.

ashley little

142

prick